'Come in,' she ▸ ... 'The water's lovely.'

He shook his head at her, amused. 'You said yourself it's not deep enough to swim in—it barely covers your feet!'

'I'm paddling,' she said, with as much dignity as was possible when she was standing in the middle of a stream. 'And it's lovely. Scared?' she taunted softly.

Slowly, with almost catlike grace, Luca pushed himself away from the tree on which he'd been leaning and leant down, loosening the ties on his boot before slipping it off, casually kicking it off his foot. His eyes fixed on Minty's face, he slid his sock off his foot, tucking it neatly into the boot. It should have looked ridiculous—*he* should have looked ridiculous. But there was something so deliberate, so assured in his movements that Minty could only stand and watch, her mouth dry.

Luca stood before her: impossibly tall, imposing. Infinitely fascinating.

'Luca...' she said hoarsely.

He didn't answer, but looked down at her searchingly. What the question was she did not know, but her face must have signalled an answer because with a muttered groan Luca pulled her close, moulding her long curves against his hard body, one hand tilting her chin up as his mouth came down upon hers.

There was nothing but him and the heat blazing between them. Nothing but the here and the now. Nothing but them.

Dear Reader

What are your most romantic memories?

Oh, bella Italia! Many years ago I visited Italy for the first time on my first holiday with my not-yet-husband. We spent the most magical week in Sorrento, walking around ancient ruins and admiring the stunning views across the incredible bay of Naples. Less than two years later we had our very own room with a view when we spent our honeymoon in Florence and the glorious Tuscan countryside.

Writing about Minty and Luca was the perfect opportunity to revisit some of my favourite places—even if it was only in my imagination! Is there anywhere more romantic than Sorrento or Florence or Rome? I couldn't think of a better setting for my wild, impetuous heroine and her childhood crush.

When socialite Minty Davenport finds herself back in the headlines and cut off from her trust fund there's only one place she can go—back to the only place she's ever called home and to the man she ran out on six years ago. Ice-cream-maker Luca Di Tore has always disapproved of the spoilt party girl; can she persuade him to give her one last chance?

Writing this book took me back to the Italy I love—to the smell of lemons in the air, the sun warming my bare arms, to seas so impossibly blue they look 'Instagrammed'. And the *food*! Trattorias selling ambrosial pizza, fresh seafood and local wines—and let's not forget the incredible *gelati*. Mine's *frutti di bosco e limone, per favore*.

I hope reading about Minty and Luca transports you to Italy too, and that you love Minty and Luca as much as I do.

Love

Jessica x

SUMMER WITH
THE MILLIONAIRE

BY
JESSICA GILMORE

Published in Great Britain 2014
by Mills & Boon, an imprint of Harlequin (UK) Limited,
Eton House, 18-24 Paradise Road, Richmond, Surrey, TW9 1SR

© 2014 Jessica Gilmore

ISBN: 978 0 263 24247 8

MORAY COUNCIL LIBRARIES & INFO.SERVICES	
20 37 18 99	
Askews & Holts	
RF RF	

After learning to read aged just two, **Jessica Gilmore** spent every childhood party hiding in bedrooms in case the birthday girl had a book or two she hadn't read yet. Discovering Mills and Boon® on a family holiday, Jessica realised that romance-writing was her true vocation and proceeded to spend her maths lessons practising her art, creating *Dynasty*-inspired series starring herself and Morten Harket's cheekbones. Writing for Mills & Boon® really is a dream come true!

A former au pair, bookseller, marketing manager and Scarborough seafront trader—selling rock from under a sign that said 'Cheapest on the Front'—Jessica now works as a membership manager for a regional environmental charity. Sadly, she spends most of her time chained to her desk, wrestling with databases, but likes to sneak out to one of their beautiful reserves whenever she gets a chance. Married to an extremely patient man, Jessica lives in the beautiful and historic city of York, with one daughter, one very fluffy dog, two dog-loathing cats and a goldfish named Bob.

On the rare occasions when she is not writing, working, taking her daughter to activities or Tweeting, Jessica likes to plan holidays—and uses her favourite locations in her books. She writes deeply emotional romance with a hint of humour, a splash of sunshine and usually a great deal of delicious food—and equally delicious heroes.

A recent book by Jessica Gilmore:

THE RETURN OF MRS JONES

This book is also available in eBook format from www.millsandboon.co.uk

For Abby

My amazing, enthusiastic, enquiring, bright girl.
Thank you for all your encouragement, belief and
pride—and thank you for just being you. I love you.

I want to thank everyone who has supported Minty,
especially my friends and colleagues who voted daily
in SYTYCW 12 and begged me not to give up. Special
thanks once again to Jane, Julia and Maggie, for reading
every single version with patience, humour and just the
occasional crack of the whip, and I owe a huge debt of
gratitude to Heidi Rice for a thoroughly comprehensive
New Writer's Scheme report—thank you.

Finally thanks to Dan for all your support x

CHAPTER ONE

'No, HE ISN'T expecting me, and no, I don't have an appointment, but...'

The impeccably made-up woman behind the desk held up a hand dismissively. 'I am sorry, *signorina*, but without an appointment I cannot let you go in.'

Minty Davenport suppressed a sigh. It was only 10:00 a.m. but she had already done more this morning than she usually managed in a full day. After negotiating the Tube armed with two large suitcases, battling the automated check-in of the budget airline and enduring her taxi driver's taste in music, she really needed something to go her way. Even the subtle scent of juniper, olives and garlic, and the sight of much missed rolling hills and olive groves, had failed to settle her nerves.

'Here is Signor Di Tore now,' the receptionist said, thankfully, gesturing to someone behind Minty. Minty closed her eyes, butterflies tumbling around her stomach.

I'm not ready for this.

But she had no choice.

Calm, collected and professional, Minty reminded herself, taking a deep breath and straightening her shoulders before pivoting round, confident smile pinned brightly onto her face.

Only to be transported back in time to her gauche teen self. To when just the sight of him had caused the breath to whoosh out of her body like a blow to the stomach—a hard blow.

Oh, he *had* changed; only for the better. She'd been hoping for seedy, balding and obese. No such luck. He was still enviably trim, but muscled in the right places. His dark hair was cut shorter than she remembered, with just enough length to run her fingers through; those strangely light caramel eyes framed by long, dark lashes. Devil's eyes, she used to taunt him.

Okay. Time to switch it on. She could do this.

'*Buongiorno*, Luca. What a beautiful day. It was so gloomy when I left London this morning, but spring seems well and truly to have hit Italy.'

Luca raised an eyebrow, laughter lurking in hooded eyes. 'I don't know what part of that statement surprises me more,' he said. 'Polite chit-chat about the weather, or the realisation that you must have got up at the crack of dawn to get here. Unless you didn't bother going to bed at all; jumped on the plane straight from one of your Mayfair nightclubs? It wouldn't be the first time,' he added.

Minty clenched her fists against the light wool of her skirt, resisting the temptation to smooth down the material. 'No, it wouldn't,' she agreed evenly. 'But you are behind the times, Luca darling; I haven't partied in Mayfair for years.' She smiled sweetly up at him. 'All the best clubs are in the east of the city now, you know. And I'm not dressed for dancing.'

Damn, she never knew when to stop talking. Why did she have to mention her clothes rather than let them make the statement for her? The laughter in Luca's eyes ratcheted up as he surveyed her up and down, the firm lips folding together to suppress something that looked suspiciously like a smile. 'So I see.'

She had dressed carefully, appropriately, in a simple grey, short-sleeved dress, a wide red belt adding a splash of colour as it cinched her narrow waist. Her shoes were a sensible height, her jewellery elegant and understated. She had even pulled her long blonde hair back into a loose bun. All she needed was a pair of glasses perched on her nose and a briefcase to make the metamorphosis complete. Leaving London in the lamplit, drizzly early hours, Minty had felt smart, professional, businesslike.

Now she felt like a child playing dress-up.

'Not that it isn't lovely to see you,' Luca continued, that same silkily sarcastic tone in his voice. 'But what have we done to deserve this rare treat? It must be at least six years since you last graced us with your presence.'

Almost exactly six years. She hadn't been back since her aunt's funeral. Since she and Luca had almost… Minty pushed the memory firmly back into its box. It wasn't relevant to today, not relevant to any day. She couldn't allow the past to derail her; couldn't afford to mess this up. 'It is the board meeting today, isn't it?' She allowed a fleeting, alarmed expression to cross her face. 'Oh, no, I didn't get the date wrong, did I?' Let him think she was unprepared. She'd show him.

'You're here for the board meeting?' Minty couldn't help feeling smug as incredulity replaced amusement. 'Why?'

'I *am* on the board,' she pointed out.

'Technically,' he said. 'But as you have never yet attended a meeting, or even sent your apologies, you'll have to forgive me for being a little confused. Have you read the papers? Do you know what's on the agenda?

I don't have time to bring you up to speed.' His tone was condescending, a little superior. Just like when they were children, when he had used every second of his four years' seniority to put her down, push her away.

She wasn't a little girl now.

Minty held up her handbag. Her prized Birkin bag had always seemed ridiculously huge, dangling off one arm with only a credit card, lipstick and mobile rattling around inside the cavernous depths. Turned out it was the perfect size for her iPad, ready-loaded not just with the last year's board-meeting papers but also Minty's notes and ideas. Her game plan. 'Read and digested.'

'Okay, then.' Luca was back to his usual inscrutable, faintly mocking self. 'I look forward to hearing your thoughts. Shall we go through?'

Hang on, this wasn't in her plan. 'What, now? The meeting doesn't start for an hour.'

'I thought you might want to settle in, freshen up.' The amber eyes gleamed. 'Prepare for the meeting. I'm sure we can find you a spare corner somewhere.'

'Thanks,' Minty said. 'But I'm quite all right here.' She gestured vaguely around the foyer. It was a light, welcoming space, the inside functional yet as lovely as the outside. Some people thought running a business the size of Di Tore Dolce from old farm buildings in the lush Oschian countryside was crazy; that they would be better moving to one of the big cities: Rome, Milan or Florence. But neither Luca nor his uncle had ever considered uprooting from the family estate where it had all begun.

The office building had once been a barn. Now it housed desks, meeting rooms and dozens of people. The reception area in which they stood was a modern, glass-roofed extension. Living vines wound abundantly round the ceiling and support beams and large wooden pots held huge, vibrant green plants. Clusters of chairs were grouped around coffee tables and to one side three smartly dressed women were seated behind a long desk. Despite the early hour, their fingers were flying away on the keyboards as they chatted into earpieces.

They were the stylish embodiment of Cerberus, the three-headed dog that guarded the entrance to Hades, and there was no getting past them. Minty had tried, unleashing the full power of her charm on them.

It hadn't worked.

On the short flight over, Minty had allowed herself a few daydreams about her successful return to Di Tore Dolce, mostly inspired by late-night *Dynasty* reruns. She would be sitting at the head of the table, presentation already set up when the other board members walked in, ready to dazzle them with her business acumen and vision.

If Cerberus hadn't barred her way.

But if Luca took her through she would immediately be sidelined, relegated back to the same position she had been in as a bored and sulky teenager dragged into the office for work experience.

Minty thought quickly. 'Honestly, you go ahead; I need to sort out my pass,' she said, darting a look over at the receptionists.

They'd have to let her through now. And then she could set up while Luca assumed she was freshening up. She could still surprise him.

'No worries, they can deliver one to you. Come on.' Luca put his hand on the small of her back and ushered Minty towards the automatic door that separated the public part of the business from the private. At just that brief contact a jolt of electricity snaked up Minty's spine and she shot forward, away from his touch.

So much for cool and professional.

But she was no longer a silly teenager with a crush. This time she was the one in control.

What on earth was Minty Davenport doing back in Oschia? And, more important, what was she doing here at Di Tore Dolce?

Luca strode over to the window and looked out over the hills and vineyards that surrounded the head office of the business he had inherited and grown. Just a mile away over the brow of the nearest hill was his home, the old Oschian farmhouse where he had lived first with his parents and then, after the accident, with his uncle, Gio, and Gio's English wife. Luca had adored the softly spoken Englishwoman—and had dreaded the summers when her wilful, wild niece came to wreak havoc for weeks on end.

Now Minty was back. What destruction did she bring in her wake this time?

And what on earth did she want with *his* business? If only Aunt Rose hadn't split her third share between the two of them; she'd given Minty a reason to return.

There had to be a reason she was back. Minty was wild, impulsive and thoughtless but her whims had never included board meetings before. Luca pulled out his phone and quickly did a search on her name. Instantly the return page showed thousands of possible hits, some dated that week. He pulled up the most recent and read, a frown pinching his forehead.

'Aha,' he said softly as he scrolled down the backlit screen. 'Got you.'

'You summoned me?' Her voice was light, full of laughter, but the blue eyes were defiant. Luca recognised the pose well: the time she'd stayed out all night... No, he corrected himself, the *times* she'd stayed out all night. After every outrageous prank, after every time she'd been called to account, Lady Araminta Davenport had presented that same mix of insouciance and bravado.

There had been a time when Luca had thought there was a vulnerability to her. That she presented a mask to the world.

He had been wrong.

Luca leant back in his chair, allowing his eyes to travel slowly down the demurely clad, long, lean body, the grey dress oddly seductive as it clung to her subtle curves. The coltish teenager had matured into a beautiful woman.

Luca looked directly at her, held her guileless gaze. 'I'm sorry to hear about your engagement.'

The blue eyes widened momentarily. A faint flush crept over her cheekbones but it was the only outward sign of any inner emotion. Surprise? Discomfort? Embarrassment? Whatever Minty was feeling, she kept it locked inside.

Once he had wanted to know—to know what she felt. To know *if* she felt. To peel back her layers and see if there was anything more to her than a trust fund with an attitude.

'To lose one fiancé is unlucky,' he said, still watching her. 'Three losses could be considered careless.'

She shrugged. 'What can I say? I never did take care of my toys.'

Had he been one of those toys? Picked up on a whim then discarded? He felt the old familiar anger rise up and swallowed it back down. He had never given her the satisfaction of reacting to her selfish and outrageous behaviour. He wasn't going to start now.

'Probably for the best. I can't really see you as a politician's wife.'

'Oh, it's not all opening fetes and kissing babies, you know; some spouses even have jobs here in the twenty-first century.' Minty wandered over to the bookshelves that lined the left side of the room and picked up a photo of her aunt. Rose was standing outside the farmhouse, her arm around a twelve-year-old Luca. He was smiling, leaning into the woman who had become his surrogate mother. He remembered that day clearly. It had been the first day since the accident that he had been happy and hadn't thought about his parents.

'It seems odd to be here, without her,' Minty said, so softly he barely made out the words. 'As the taxi drove past the house, I half-expected it to turn in to the driveway and I'd see her standing on the step in that flour-covered apron of hers.' She put the photo down and continued to browse along the shelves, examining the photos and awards he kept there.

For a moment Luca softened. Rose had been just as much Minty's surrogate mother as his; it must be strange for her to be back in Oschia for the first time since the funeral. But it had been her choice to stay away; to run away in the middle of the night; to barely bother keeping in touch with Uncle Gio, the man who had provided her with stability and a home for over ten summers.

'It says here that your father wasn't very pleased about the engagement being called off.'

Minty turned, leaning back against the bookshelves, confident, graceful, unpredictable as a cat. 'You shouldn't read gossip websites, they're very bad for you.'

'Ah, but how else would we know what you are up to?'

Her eyes gleamed. 'I didn't know you cared.'

Luca stared at her, not trying to hide his contempt. 'I don't, but Gio worries about you. Is it true?'

Minty wandered back towards the desk, dropping into the chair opposite, folding one long leg over the other as she did so. 'True that Daddy was unhappy? You know Daddy. Inconvenient offspring of early marriages should not be seen, not be heard and definitely not be splashed all over the newspapers. He was a tad cross.'

'Is that why you're here?'

She gave him a long look from under her lashes. 'Can't you just believe that I was seized with a desire to contribute to the company?'

A burst of impatience shot through him. She'd been back for less than an hour and already she was playing games, turning his plans upside down. No way was he allowing her into that board meeting without knowing exactly why she was here and what she wanted. 'Come on, Minty,' he said. 'You may be a shareholder, but as we plough most of the profits back into expansion we can only be a tiny part of your income.' His eyes slid to the snakeskin Birkin bag dumped by the door. 'A tiny part,' he repeated. 'You have never shown any interest in Di Tore Dolce before. Why now?'

Minty was silent for a long moment; he could see the wheels turning in her mind as she considered his question, considered how much to reveal. Finally she seemed to come to a decision. 'I need a job,' she said.

For a moment Minty thought Luca was going to laugh at her but the laughter quickly faded from his eyes, his mouth twisting sceptically as he took in her words.

The silence dragged on a second too long. Minty

forced herself to stay relaxed, leaning back in her chair, her face calm, impassive.

After all, how many times could this man reject her?

Finally, just as her nerves wound tighter than her mother's last facelift, he spoke. 'Do you have a CV?'

'With me, or at all? Not that it matters; I don't have one.'

Luca had looked relaxed, in control, ever since she had walked into his office, leaning back in that ridiculously big chair. Now he sat up and leaned forward, eyes fixed on her face. 'You are asking me for a job but you don't have a CV?' he repeated slowly.

Minty toyed with the idea of pointing out that, with a sixth share of the business, asking Luca was merely a formality, but one look at the stony expression on his face told her winding him up further was probably a bad idea. Shame; it would have been fun. He had always been so easy to rile.

And he was easier to handle when he was cross with her. Less dangerous.

'I've never needed one before; I never had to formally apply for anything,' she said. 'But I *do* have a lot of varied experience. I've crewed a boat halfway around the world, run a Greek taverna, taught English in Bangkok and was a cow girl in Texas for a while.' She smiled at him. 'I'm aware none of these are particularly relevant but—'

'Relevant to what?' Luca interrupted. 'Sales, finance, reception, milk maid?' To Minty's indignation the amusement was back in his voice. Damn; she had tried so hard not to be alone with him before the meeting because she knew he would be like this: superior; condescending. He wouldn't hear her out.

It was all too familiar. She carried on as if he hadn't

spoken. 'But they do show that I am adaptable, versatile and not afraid of hard work. I know you think it's time for Di Tore Dolce to expand beyond the continent, into the English-speaking countries. I'm half-American and half-English—I can help you see the real differences in the two markets beyond the superficial accent and spelling differences. Also, don't forget I founded a small cupcake chain in West London. I know all about stock management, sales and marketing. Oh, and budgeting too.'

She sat back, ankles crossed, hands folded in her lap. Excitement fizzed in her veins; she had said her piece, made her pitch. Had shown that she was abreast of current plans and developments. And in stark contrast to a minute ago Luca was looking engaged, interested.

He remained silent for a moment, a thoughtful expression on his face. She tried not to stare at him hopefully, to appear nonchalant, relaxed.

As if this didn't really matter at all.

And then he leant back again. 'If you have a business back in England why do you need a job here?'

And just like that her mood went flat. 'England and I need a break from each other,' Minty said.

'Come on, Minty. You need to do better than that.'

Only four years older. And yet he had always acted as if he were an adult and she an annoying child. She suppressed a scowl. It looked like nothing had changed. 'Three cupcake shops in South London is fun but Di Tore Dolce is in a different league altogether. You're already international; if the board goes ahead with the expansion, you'll be close to global. Who wouldn't want to be part of that?'

Luca raised an eyebrow. 'Such enthusiasm from somebody who has been absent for so long the receptionists didn't even recognise her. Are you sure you wouldn't rather be expanding your cupcake empire?'

'Quite sure,' Minty said. 'Besides, the shops were funded through my trust fund. I am trying to rely on it less.'

That was one way of putting it.

His brows drew together, puzzled. 'You are?' He looked pointedly again at her expensive bag, his eyes travelling to her equally expensive shoes. 'How novel for you. Inspiring, even. Unless…' There was a speculative gleam in the amber eyes. 'Unless you *can't* rely on it. Just how upset was your father?'

Minty mentally went through the weapons at her disposal and dismissed them all. She doubted he'd be moved by tears, nor impressed with flirtation. There was no way she was going to plead.

She'd have to settle for honesty.

She looked down at her right hand and twisted the moonstone ring she wore on her middle finger round and round. Her left hand felt bare; yet another engagement ring removed. She'd liked the latest one too—not big, not ostentatious, not a family heirloom.

She took a deep breath. Right, honesty. How hard could it be? She looked back up, directly at Luca. 'Daddy was furious,' she said. 'Not that he particularly liked Joe, but he wanted me settled. And he hated the publicity. Although I think that's more because the press always drag up his three divorces, which kind of bursts his "happy family" bubble. Anyway, he decided I needed some tough love and cutting off my trust fund was the kindest thing he could do. Because I used my trust fund to start the first shop, he banned me from entering the premises. Too easy, he said.'

It took some work to keep the bitterness from her

voice. *Tough love.* That was a good one. It would have been nice if he'd tried unconditional love first.

'So you came to us in desperation?' Luca said drily.

Ouch, that cut far too close. 'Oh, no,' Minty assured him, making sure she kept her voice light and breezy, not letting him see how much she wanted this, needed this. 'Desperation would have meant accepting one of the reality TV shows I keep being offered, or pretending to write a book. And there are a lot of art galleries who would snap me up. Pearls, a little black dress and an expensive education are all they require, and I have all three in abundance. But, believe it or not, I want more; I do always read the board's papers. I think this expansion is a good idea, and I want to be part of it.'

Minty put as much conviction as possible into her voice.

'I'm glad our plans have your approval.' Why did he have to sound so scathing? 'But your sudden desire to contribute still seems a little suspicious. After all, apart from collecting your annual cheque, you haven't shown any interest in Di Tore Dolce—or Oschia—for years. And now you want to…what? To move here? Or do you see your role as being more ambassadorial? Wining and dining prospective clients? Parties?'

Minty bit her lip. This was what she'd been afraid of—her plans dismissed out of hand, her ideas rejected unheard. And now she was here, actually back in Oschia, she was suddenly unsure. After all, he had shown her more than once how little he valued her. That he thought her nothing but a spoilt child.

He wasn't the only one who thought that, yet somehow, even now, his disapproval stung that little bit more.

She stared unseeingly out of the window, at the landscape that used to feel like home. It hadn't been for a long, long time. Maybe she *should* go back to London. Stop fighting her birthright, her destiny. Take a job in a West End gallery and share a flat with one of her trust-afarian friends. Rejoin society—go to Henley, Ascot, shooting parties and hunt balls; see if she could attract the kind of husband who asked for little more than the right family and the ability to throw a good party. She'd managed it once, after all. Maybe this time she could actually go through with the wedding.

'No, I want more than that.' The conviction in her voice surprised her, and she could see Luca looked taken aback too. 'I know this seems like a whim to you. And it *is* sudden. But I *have* thought it through; I've planned a role which fits in with the board's objectives.'

'Come on, Minty.' Luca pushed his chair back and got up, walking over to the window and looking out. He stood there for one long moment then turned back to face her. 'You can't just swan in after all these years and expect us to fit in around your half-baked ideas. You've read the papers? Great. You're a shareholder; you *should* know what's going on. But that doesn't mean that because you are bored with your shallow London life you can create a job here. We need people we can rely on, not people who run away in the middle of the night without even leaving a note.'

The room seemed distant, fuzzy. Her stomach churned as heat enveloped her, her palms clammy, her throat dry. Minty opened her mouth and then shut it. What could she say? She couldn't believe he was even *mentioning* that night.

After all, she had spent six years trying to forget every single second of it.

But there was no way she was going to let Luca Di Tore know just how his actions had affected her.

She barely admitted it to herself.

Minty lifted her chin and looked directly at him, as if it didn't matter at all. 'I was young, Luca. Scared. Grieving. I didn't know what I was doing.'

Hadn't known what *they* were doing. Hadn't known how her childhood adversary had suddenly become someone she was so, so tempted to cling to. Someone she needed. Wanted. Trusted.

He'd soon proved her wrong.

'Not that young, Minty. You were engaged a month later. That was your first engagement, I believe,' he added.

Minty swallowed a half-hysterical giggle. As if her engagement to Barty could be compared to what had nearly happened with Luca. Barty had been safe, undemanding, still a boy. She hadn't needed him, hadn't expected anything from him other than fun and flirtation.

She had wanted everything from Luca.

Until the moment he'd pushed her away. Until she had looked up to see nothing but horror in his eyes.

She pushed the unwanted memories away. She needed this to work; needed to find out if she was anything more than a pretty face and an old name, more than a trust-fund baby with a tabloid-friendly romantic history. 'Rose wanted me to be part of the business,' she said softly. 'That was why she left me half her share.'

Luca stared back, indecision in his eyes. She knew he wanted nothing more than to give her her marching orders, put her back on a plane and order her to never set foot in Oschia again. But she had played her trump card, gambled it all on his sense of honour, his respect for the woman who had raised him.

He shut his eyes then they snapped open, all indecision gone. 'Okay,' Luca said. 'You have two weeks.

Two weeks to show me you can do the job. If you do, you can stay.'

Jubilation filled her. He was giving her a chance. Minty jumped to her feet and ran round the desk, flinging her arms around the tall figure. 'Thank you,' she said. 'Thank you, you won't regret it.' She leant in, her face pressed against the cotton of his shirt, and before she could stop herself she inhaled. The fresh fragrance of his clean shirt mingled with the sharp freshness of his aftershave, mixed up with something warm, spicy. Something uniquely male. The smell shot through her, sending a jolt of sensual awareness right down to her toes.

She was all too aware of him, of the muscles under her hands, of his height, his strength. The leg pressed against hers, the flatness of his belly. If she raised her head just a little, she knew her mouth would be tantalisingly close to the pulse at his throat.

What was she doing? She dropped her hands and stumbled back.

He was as still as the Renaissance statue he resembled. His was face unreadable, his eyes shuttered.

Minty swallowed and moistened her lips. 'It means a lot,' she said. 'Your faith.'

'Don't get carried away.' She flinched. Was that a reference to her inappropriate bodily contact? 'I have very little faith in you. And don't think you can just start at the top. I served an apprenticeship here while you lazed by the pool and chatted up all the local boys. I have worked in every single department, from deliveries to stock management, learned how everything works. You'll do the same over the next two weeks. One bad report, just one, and it's all over. You sell your shares back to me and never come near me or my company again. Is that understood?'

A gamble. This was Minty's language. Her ancestors had won—and lost—fortunes on the turn of a dice or a card. A Davenport never refused a wager. And they always played to win.

'Understood,' she said, holding her hand out to him. 'We have a deal. If I lose, you buy my share at full market price, not a penny less. Not that I intend to lose.' She grinned, all her old confidence rushing back. This was a challenge she could sink her teeth into. This was going to be fun.

'In that case...' Luca's expression gave nothing away. 'We'd better go and introduce you to the board. After all, many of them have no idea who you are. If you're ready?' He gestured to the door, keeping a clear distance between them.

Maybe he had been more affected by their brief contact than he had let on.

Or maybe he just didn't want her to embarrass herself again. He really didn't need to worry. That lesson had been well and truly learned.

'Ready.' She walked over to the door and picked up her bag, swinging it jauntily from her arm. This was it. 'Just one more thing—I haven't got anywhere to stay, and I'm a little short of cash and credit, which is less fun than I imagined. Could I stay in my old room at the farmhouse? Just for a few weeks? It's what Rose would have wanted,' she added, perhaps unwisely.

Luca moved so fast she barely saw him towering over her, his body between hers and the room. He put both hands on the wall either side of her, pinning her in place. 'Don't push me, Minty,' he warned, his voice low and gravelly, the accent more pronounced than ever. 'Don't ever try to play me again. Consider this a warning.'

She was momentarily paralysed by his proximity; by the heat burning in the molten gold of his eyes; by her body's traitorous reaction to his display of strength. But she was older, if not wiser; stronger. She summoned up all her attitude and stared brazenly back at him, a smile playing on her lips. 'I take it that's a no?'

He released her abruptly. 'Your room is still as you left it. Gio insisted. You tidy up after yourself, you cook for yourself and you stay out of my way. Clear?'

'As crystal,' she said.

She gathered up her bag and followed him meekly out of the room, trying not to let her eyes linger on the length of his legs, the power in his stride. She had two weeks to work hard and keep her head down.

It had to be enough. She couldn't afford to lose. Not this time.

CHAPTER TWO

LUCA WATCHED MINTY as she preceded him into the boardroom. He had seen her in many guises but this prim, butter-wouldn't-melt look was a new one to him. And to her too, he thought, noticing her hands pull nervously at her skirt, rising to her head as she fiddled with the neat bun her usually flowing hair was pinned back in. Her demeanour might be cool and collected but she was nervous.

What on earth did she have to be nervous about? What was she planning?

She had her two weeks, didn't she? What else did she need?

The large room was still empty. Adapted from an old hay loft, it had huge skylights all along the slanting roof allowing the morning light to flood in. The west wall was a lightly tinted screen of glass, shielding eyes from the bright sun whilst allowing those inside to admire the pastoral view beyond. The back wall was timber and brick and hung all over with posters from old advertising campaigns. One half of the room was taken up with a traditional oval wooden conference-table, large enough to sit twenty, the other half with comfortable chairs and sofas for more informal gatherings. Today's meeting would begin with coffee and chat as usual, and the cups and steaming jugs were already laid out, along with plates of breakfast pastries, fresh fruit and a variety of other snacks.

One plate really stood out amongst the more traditional pastries, rolls and cheeses: a chilled platter of tiny frozen spheres in a variety of pinks, creams and reds. Luca watched in amusement as Minty picked up a particularly inviting-looking pink and cream affair and popped it into her mouth with a fervent, 'Oh, good, food. I'm starving.'

He waited. It didn't take long.

'*Eurgh.*' Looking about her wildly, Minty groped for a napkin and inelegantly spat out the remains of the canapé into its white folds. 'That's not strawberries and cream! Or if it is there is something seriously wrong with your recipes, Luca.'

'No,' he said, trying without much success to keep his face straight. 'We usually have a tasting session before each meeting. This is our new line of canapés: frozen savouries. That one, I believe, was smoked salmon and cream cheese.'

'That explains the fishy aftertaste,' Minty said, her face still screwed up in disgust.

'Try it again,' he said, picking up another pink and cream canapé and offering it to her. 'Now you know what it is, see what you think of the flavours.'

'What's wrong with a nice blini? Some fresh black pepper, a dollop of sour cream, just a hint of lemon: there's a reason it's a classic,' Minty grumbled but took the ball cautiously between her finger and thumb and nibbled at it. Her face gradually relaxed as she savoured the taste and she took a larger bite. 'Now I know what it is, it isn't bad,' she said. 'Subtle. Texture's nice too, not slimy. How did you manage that? What are the other flavours?'

'The red one is tomato mixed with ciabatta crumb, the pale pink one ham, parmesan and caramelised onion. Try one.'

'People will seriously buy this stuff?' Minty picked up the ham and parmesan and sniffed it gingerly. 'I mean, I like a nice Earl Grey sorbet as much as the next girl, but savoury ice-cream canapés?'

'You are behind the times, Araminta *cara*.' Luca popped one of the icy tomato balls into his mouth and tasted the sharp, sweet hit of tomato, the herby crumbs tempering the sweetness. Delicious. It had taken months to get the texture right, not so sloppy a sorbet that it couldn't be finger food, nor so creamy that it over-shadowed the taste. 'Food experimentation, playing with perceptions, sweet and savoury combinations, is huge right now; this product allows any party-giver to show how modern and sophisticated they are. How-ever, a girl whose idea of a perfect meal is a fishfinger sandwich can't be expected to appreciate something so adventurous.' He waited, an eyebrow raised, for the inevitable reaction.

'Actually...' Luca grinned as Minty rose to the bait just as he had known she would. Some things never changed. 'I think you'll find that fish goujons served with rocket, aioli and ciabatta is a staple in any self-respecting gastro-pub.'

He repressed a shudder. 'And that is why I will never eat in England.'

'Snob.'

'Philistine.'

The tension crackled between them. Minty was stand-ing close, so close it would take less than a second to pull her to him, to silence her the only way that had ever proved effective. The blood thrummed in his ears as his eyes fastened on the full curve of her mouth, wide, provocative, tempting.

It would be a lie to say that the memory of kissing Minty Davenport had haunted him for the past six years; a lie to say that he had wasted those years yearning to taste her again. And yet the oddest things would remind him of that night; remind him how gloriously right it had felt, how right she had felt.

How right *they* had felt, as if all the years of competition and antagonism had led them to this point.

But she had been too young. Grieving. He couldn't, he wouldn't, have taken advantage of that. Of her. Stopping might have been hard but it had been the right thing to do.

And in the morning she had gone. No note; no word for six long years. Until today, waltzing in as if she had never been away, as unpredictable, as selfish, as ever.

And just because the memory of that night, that kiss, hung heavily in the atmosphere didn't mean he had to act on it. Not at all.

Luca had a plan for his future, for his business, for his home. Minty didn't figure anywhere.

Just two weeks and she would be gone. He needed to keep his distance and never, ever let himself forget who and what she was.

It was time for him to take control.

Fifteen minutes later the room was filled with the remaining board members. Luca, his Uncle Gio and Minty were the only stockholders. Having taken up the reins at such a young age, Luca had carried on with Gio's practice of having an independent board made up of professionals with very different skills, from an expert in international law, whose only connection with Di Tore Dolce was these meetings, to Giovanna, a woman in her early sixties who had made *gelato* for the Di Tores since her teens.

He might not always take their advice but he valued it.

The meeting began informally, as always, and the room was filled with the usual hubbub of chit-chat, greetings and animated conversation as the board members caught up whilst sampling the food on offer. With one eye on the clock, Luca managed to back Minty into a corner, keeping her engaged in conversation and making it hard for her to mingle. By the time the others had taken their places at the table, she was well and truly relegated to the position of visitor, the object of everyone's gaze and curiosity.

Thank goodness Gio was running late; he would have swept her into the midst of the conversation before Luca could say *'ciao'.*

'Everyone,' Luca said in English, 'I would like to introduce Araminta Davenport. Although you may not know her by sight…' He bestowed a smile on the silently fulminating Minty. *That was right; mark her out as an outsider from the off.* 'You may be aware that she was left a sixth of the company by my aunt. It's lovely to see her take an interest in the company at last. Come on, Minty, let's find you a seat.'

Luca took care to spend some time ensuring she was comfortable, deliberately continuing to emphasise her visitor status. 'Would you rather we held the meeting in English?' he asked solicitously and had the pleasure of seeing her practically bare her teeth at him as she assured him that, really, her Italian was quite adequate, thank you.

One-nil to Luca.

Over the next half-hour Luca almost forgot that Minty was in the room. Almost. The occasional glance of her neatly coiffed head nodding earnestly as someone made a valid point; the sight of her typing rapid notes onto her iPad; the small wrinkle at the bridge of her nose when the conversation became more animated or technical than her rusty Italian could follow would make him falter, check his notes, regroup.

But so far she had said nothing. Not even a murmur of agreement. Luca felt the slight weight of worry lift. Maybe she was just here to observe; maybe he had seen trouble where there was none.

The niceties were soon dealt with: apologies, minutes, agendas, a few small points all despatched. It was time for the main event.

It was time to address the international expansion, the biggest change to Di Tore Dolce since they had made the decision to produce not just the traditional *gelato* but the full range of Italian desserts. And this expansion was all Luca's.

He pressed a button on his laptop and pulled up the presentation, adrenaline flooding through his veins. The business was profitable, successful and flourishing under his leadership despite the difficult financial conditions. It was time to take it global. He smiled confidently at the table and opened his mouth, ready to begin. But before he could speak the first carefully prepared word, the door opened.

Gio had arrived, smiling, full of apologies, bestowing embraces all round. Minty rose to her feet, ready for his embrace as he walked in, but Luca could tell that

behind her smile and hug she was shocked. Shocked at
how the bear of a man had shrunk, at the lines on his
face, the greyness of his hair. Shocked that the twinkle
in his eyes was just a faded reflection of the real thing.
Luca recognised the shock; he felt it too every time he
saw his uncle.

When Rose had died, Gio's heart had died too.

What did that feel like, to be halved like that? Luca
knew what he wanted and it wasn't such grand emotion, such all-or-nothing passion.

He wanted compatibility, comfort.

Almost against his will, his glance slid over to Minty,
still enfolded in Gio's arms. Resolutely Luca wrenched
his eyes away again.

Minty was many things but she had never been comfortable.

'Okay, everyone.' It was time to call this meeting
back to order. 'Gio, lovely to see you.' He tried not to
allow the anxiety his uncle's appearance caused him
to show in his voice. Was he eating enough? Drinking too much?

When would he stop grieving for a woman who had
been dead for six years?

'As you know, I have been investigating expanding
into some of the English-speaking territories,' he began,
projecting confidence as he spoke, looking round the
table to catch and hold every single person's eye. They
were all nodding and smiling back at him. All except
Minty, who was frowning down at her iPad. A surge
of irritation ran through him. She had seemed so keen
on the expansion back in his office.

Instantly heat flamed through his body as the memory of her impulsive embrace hit him: the lean length

of her, impossibly, incredibly soft; the way she fit into him, around him.

Luca took a hurried gulp of water.

He took care to avoid looking at Minty as he carried on, spending the next twenty minutes taking the board through the figures, projections and risk analysis of the project. They seemed engaged, approving. And so they should; Luca had been working on this for months.

'Any questions?' he finished. There were just a few hands: some clarifications, double-checking of the figures; nothing major, nothing to worry about.

And why would there be?

'Bene.' He beamed round at the assembled company. 'If we are all agreed, then…'

'I'm sorry.' Luca looked up in shock. She chose to speak now?

'Si?' he bit out impatiently.

Minty smiled apologetically but those blue eyes were steely. Whatever she intended, she planned to see through. The long-buried antagonism began to force its way back into Luca's consciousness. What act of sabotage was she plotting?

'I have something to say. There's actually a presentation.' She gestured towards the iPad. 'Do you all mind?'

'Of course not,' Gio broke in. 'Help Minty set up, Luca. Let's hear what she has to say.'

Lips set, mind whirling furiously, Luca obeyed. To shut her down would seem churlish, as if he had something to hide. The cunning little minx: she had set him up. The clothes, the lowered eyelashes, the hair—it was all an act, just as he had guessed. Of course, he thought darkly, the leopard doesn't change its spots.

But what did this particular feline want this time and, more importantly, what did she want with his company?

* * *

Minty's pulse was racing, her palms slippery with nervous sweat as she stood up and walked towards the head of the table, putting as confident a swagger into her walk as she could manage.

She couldn't let him shut her down. Not this time.

It had taken six years, three broken engagements and the loss of everything to bring her back here. But, now she *was* back, she suddenly, desperately, wanted to succeed. Needed to succeed.

She needed to show Luca she was worth more than a quiet 'no'.

She needed to show herself that she was worth something. Worth anything.

One of her ex-fiancés was a musician; another a politician. They had nothing in common apart from having presented Minty with an engagement ring and then telling her she could keep it, a last act of patronising kindness as they'd walked away. But both men knew how to work a crowd. Very different crowds, true, but they both had the knack of commanding the attention of everyone in the room with the sheer power of their personality.

It was all in the presentation.

And confidence. 'If you believe you can do it,' Joe had said, 'anything is possible.' The trite, predictable sound bite of a politician, but Minty was going to take his words at face value.

She could do this.

'Buongiorno,' she said and, taking a leaf out of Luca's book, she smiled around the table, making sure she caught every single person's eye before she moved on. Even Luca's, although it took every ounce of determination she had to meet that burningly intense gaze.

His eyes were smouldering gold, promising slow, painful retribution. Just like the time she borrowed his rare Batman comic and dropped it in the swimming pool. Not entirely by accident.

Enough dwelling on the past; this was about the here and now. About impressing them, proving that she had a right to be here; that despite everything she belonged.

'Expanding into the UK is a great idea,' she began smoothly, pulling up her first slide as she spoke. 'As you can see, the UK has been getting more and more serious about food over the last couple of decades with a much bigger variation in both restaurant types and meals cooked at home. Traditional Italian ingredients such as pasta are now a British staple.'

She gave a quick smile to hide her nerves. Gio caught her eye and gave her a broad wink of approval and Minty's spirits rose. She didn't sound like an idiot.

Confidence buoyed, she carried on, taking them through statistics on British dietary habits, eating-out spend and grocery spend. Luca lounged back in his chair, the anger in his eyes simmering down to annoyance. So far she was covering no new ground.

Minty was fully aware of that.

'The expansion as it stands is a two-pronged plan,' she said. This was it, when she deviated from the ideas and costings Luca had put together. Butterflies tumbled through her stomach, making it hard to catch her breath. 'Restaurants and specialist food-outlets. I'm not going to discuss restaurants, as they buy different quantities and are sold differently, but I am going to tell you why I think focussing on the specialist outlets is a mistake.'

The challenge was thrown down.

Minty didn't intend to look at Luca at this point but she felt his gaze on her and, like a magnet, it drew her in. He was no longer leaning back, no longer simmering. He sat bolt-upright, those disquieting eyes fixed on her face, a tiger ready to pounce. Her mouth dry, she carried on, moistening her lips with her tongue, resisting the instincts that screamed at her to back away slowly. To stop right now.

Too bad she always ignored her instincts.

'Supplying ready-made *gelato* and Italian-made puddings to the UK *is* the right course,' she said. 'Although we love to talk about cooking, to watch cooking programmes and to buy vast libraries of cookbooks, most people in the UK don't really enjoy cooking. Not day-to-day. Or people are too just too busy to cook properly. Also, at weekends they feel like they deserve a treat, a break from the kitchen, but the recession has meant that the old staples of going out or ordering takeaways are no longer weekly treats but monthly indulgences.'

Minty took a deep breath. 'This in turn has given rise to the gourmet ready-meal. Dine in for ten pounds for two, or kits that you put together in your kitchen and that take five minutes to cook but make you feel like you actually made the meal.'

There were a few murmurs at this. Minty looked round the incredulous-looking people who sat opposite her and had to restrain a laugh. They could as little comprehend a world where people bought their lasagne ready-made as they could imagine a talking dog. Which was exactly why they needed her; they just didn't know it yet.

'Some gourmet food shops do provide ready meals,' she continued. 'But the people who shop there have different values. They care about food, which is great for us, but they also care about origin. A York deli will want to sell ice cream made with cream from Yorkshire cows, not Italian cows, to cut down on food miles and support local economies. And the food miles *will* be exorbitant; supplying a few delis here and there will cost a fortune, eating into our margins.'

Minty took a deep breath. The table was silent, every person hanging on her every word. Excitement surged but she ruthlessly dampened it down. She wasn't there yet.

'One solution would be to concentrate on London, which has a huge amount of delis and a sizeable Italian population. But then we haven't really tapped into the UK, just a tiny part of it.

'So we should consider the supermarkets.'

There. It was said.

There was a stunned silence. Minty pressed on, 'Not every supermarket, not even the most popular super-markets, but the most *up-market* supermarkets, to fit in with the aspirational and fresh appeal of the brand. There are two who will manage our prices, sell-by dates and image without cheapening and demeaning our brand. Their endorsement will make us desirable to the delis and specialist food-outlets you prefer and, crucially, raise our profile with the consumer.'

Minty looked up at the last slide, a stock image of a laughing, loving nuclear family gathered around a table, bowls of ice cream in front of them.

What would it be like to be part of such a family?

She thrust the thought aside and lifted her chin. 'Any questions?'

She risked a look over at Luca's chair opposite. He was leaning back again, relaxed. To all appearances, open to ideas and opinions.

Unless you looked closely at his eyes. A chill shivered down Minty's spine. She was no coward but she couldn't sustain eye contact of any length with such contemptuous anger blazing out at her. She wanted to challenge him, to sustain the advantage her height and position gave her as she stood at the front of his boardroom, but she quailed before him and lowered her eyelids, blocking out the unleashed fury.

Submitting.

Idiot; coward, she admonished herself. *You have a right to be here, to make your point.*

But when she steeled herself to take him back on, plastered on her most guileless expression and raised innocent eyes back to his face, it was too late. His expression was bland, his eyes hooded. Emotionless.

Maybe she had made up the earlier anger, seen only what she was expecting to see. But the hairs still stood up on her arms; a disquieting prickle at the back of her neck was a reminder. Luca could have been a formidable ally. Instead she had made a dangerous enemy.

There was no time to dwell on her tactics as the questions began. If Minty had thought she could get away with making her presentation unchallenged, she was wrong. The board members might not have had a chance to prepare their questions but that didn't stop them. Which supermarkets? Prices, margins, market penetration, rival brands? Minty had done her homework, had spent the past two weeks preparing, but the level of detail they wanted at this stage astonished her. Frightened her.

It was very different from sitting down with the three women who managed her cupcake cafés. From the cosy chats over coffee and cakes about new recipes, promotions, staff. Her accountant took care of the finances, the staff the social media and marketing. The shop managers were responsible for all the day-to-day issues.

She was just a trust-fund baby with a vanity business, after all.

The door was so close. She could just leave, sell the damn shares. With the money she could travel, start again, open up a new vanity project: design handbags, maybe, like many a socialite before her. She wouldn't need her trust fund.

But Aunt Rose had left her the shares. She had believed in Minty, had wanted her to be involved. She had never believed Minty could let her down, would let her down. Maybe she'd been the only person who had ever believed that?

'Don't fudge; if you don't know the answer, say you'll find out and get back to them. Always get back to them. And never let them see you're scared.' Who would have thought that Joe's 'top ten tips on winning over the electorate' would come in so handy? Minty squared her shoulders, turned her charm up full blast and answered the questions as best she could, as confidently as she could.

And she *was* winning them over; she could see it in their eyes, their demeanour.

Of course, not everyone was getting carried away. 'Have you set up meetings with these supermarkets? Discussed pricing, volume and distribution?' Luca, the voice of reason: cold, questioning, eyes narrowed, pen poised over paper, waiting for her answer. Like a headmaster dealing with a disappointing pupil.

'Not yet. It seemed premature.' Minty had considered it. She had gone as far as finding out the names of the buyers involved, but making the next step scared her. She repressed a shudder, imagining herself there like an *Apprentice* contestant, trying to convince the supermarkets to buy. What if she overpitched or under-pitched?

What if she cost the company hundreds of thousands by negotiating too low a discount—or lost the opportunity by going in too high?

Maybe this idea of Luca's that she spend two weeks learning the ropes had some merit after all.

Merit beyond proving him wrong, that was.

'That sounds eminently sensible.' The sound of Gio's voice made her jump. He'd been silent up to now, she realised with a sense of shock. The Gio she remembered was larger than life in business, in laughter, in food, in love. Not a man to sit quietly and listen, his eyes troubled and sad. 'I think Minty has made her case very well. Now it's up to us to investigate the feasibility, with Minty's input, of course. You are planning to stay, aren't you?'

Minty opened her mouth to assure him that, yes, she was planning to stay for the time being—noncommittal agreement, her speciality. But something in his eyes made her stop. 'I hope to,' she said, surprising herself by the honesty in her voice. 'I mean, I'd like to.'

'Good.' Gio sat up a little straighter and turned to Luca. 'In that case, fifty per cent of the shareholders are in favour of advancing Minty's idea to the next stage. Are you going to make it one hundred percent or will we need to put it to the board?'

It wasn't anger in Luca's eyes now, or contempt. It was shock. Of course, Minty thought. As a fifty per cent shareholder and CEO he had the majority vote. It was only her presence that made a tie possible. For six years he had had things all his own way.

Minty had just spoiled all his fun.

'There's no harm in investigating,' he said slowly. 'I'll talk to our head of sales later today.' He shot a glance at Minty. 'You'll need to be there.'

'Of course.'

'It's just an investigation at this stage,' he warned them. 'It may not be feasible. But we'll look into it. Okay, if there are no more questions on the expansion, let's move on. Giovanna, I believe the next section is yours...'

There was no time to talk to Minty alone after the meeting. It wasn't until Luca's head of sales had left his office, armed with the relevant information, that Luca was able to catch her. 'Just a minute, Minty,' he said, his voice deceptively calm. 'I just want a quick word.'

She was already at the door, holding on to the handle as if it were her only hope. As well she might, he thought grimly. Luckily for Minty, several hours had given him the chance to cool down. A little bit.

'Sit down,' he invited, still silkily calm. For a moment he thought she might defy him, insist on standing just because she could, just because she was Minty Davenport and always had to be contrary. But, after a long moment's silent contemplation, she folded herself gracefully into a chair, limpid eyes fixed on his.

He continued to look at her levelly and had the satisfaction of seeing her squirm under his regard. Minty loved a bit of drama; a good argument didn't faze her at all. But the silent treatment, ignoring her? That had always proved far more effective.

'Gio's offered to give me a lift back to the house,' she said at last, caving in, breaking the silence first. 'He's going to let me have his keys for now, and he still has your old Fiat, which he's happy for me to borrow while I'm here. I wouldn't want to be dependent on you—I mean, I'm sure you would find that annoying.'

'He's pleased to see you. He always wanted you to

be involved.' The rebuke was subtle but as pointed as he could make it, and by the flush that crept over her cheeks it had hit home.

Good.

'It's lovely to see him, although a bit of a shock; he seems so much older.' An anxious expression shadowed her face. 'In some ways I barely recognised him. Is he okay?'

Luca didn't reply. If she really cared about Gio she would have written. Or phoned, emailed, faxed, texted, tweeted. In this day and age there were no excuses for six years' silence. She could have hauled her party-going ass onto a plane and come to visit. The righteous anger fuelled him, made it easy to ignore the concern in her eyes.

'I don't know why you are here or what you want,' he said finally. 'Regardless of your little stunt in the boardroom, my conditions still stand. I have your schedule here.' He passed her a sheet of paper and she took it wordlessly, her blue eyes huge as she stared across at him. She looked tired, vulnerable, every bit the penniless adventurer who had risen at the crack of dawn to try to seek out her fortune.

She was quite the actress.

'I'm sorry if you didn't like what I had to say—' she began. Luca cut her off ruthlessly.

'No you're not.'

She blinked at him. 'Not what?'

'You're not sorry. Not at all. You wanted to come in here and make a big splash. Minty Davenport wins the day. Your clothes, your hair...' His words were tumbling out now in anger, frustration, all the negative emotions this dammed woman stirred up in him. 'It's just the same as when we were kids. You always had some new role, some new drama. Remember the summer you decided to be an eco-warrior? Lectured us the whole time on our food, our cars, our clothes. Then you turned up again nine months later, clad in leather and guzzling up as much hot water as possible.'

'I was fifteen...'

'Your artist stage,' he continued ruthlessly. 'How much did you spend on lessons and supplies? I bet you haven't picked up a brush in years.'

'That has got nothing to do with—'

'And this is your latest fantasy: running a company, making presentations, wearing a suit and coming into an office every day? Not in my company, Minty. I will not allow my hard work to be a backdrop for your latest role. I will not allow it.'

When had he risen to his feet? Leant over his desk? Why was it he only lost control of his emotions when she was around? Luca took a deep breath, tried to still the adrenaline swirling around his body, the blood thumping in his ears. She was staring at him, eyes still wide but now with shock. 'Your points were valid, Minty,' he said more calmly. 'If you had come to me earlier, told me your thoughts, I would have listened, incorporated them. We could have gone to the board together with a final plan, costings. You didn't need to make such a drama out of it. You don't need to make such a drama out of everything.'

Were those tears swimming in her eyes? She blinked rapidly and the shine was gone. Maybe he'd imagined it, had seen what he wanted to see.

She had always played him—as a child, a teenager. It looked like nothing had changed. 'It ends here,' he added more calmly. 'Understand? Or you can leave right away. You have something to say? Talk to me. Work with me. I'm open to suggestion, ask anyone.'

His eyes continued to bore into her, to pin her down. 'But if it's not business then I don't want to hear it. Gio may be glad you're back.' He leaned on his desk, eyes boring into hers. 'But I'm not. Stay out of my way, Minty. That's a warning.'

CHAPTER THREE

EVERY LIMB WAS HEAVY; her head was not just foggy but filled with a traditional London pea-souper straight from the nineteen-thirties. Minty wasn't sure she could even stagger down the driveway, let alone open the front door and flop her exhausted body inside when she got there.

'Ciao, Gianni; ciao Alfonso. Grazie; a presto,' she said, feebly pushing the heavy lorry door shut, managing a small wave at the grinning drivers as she did so. How did they manage to stay awake? And so cheerful. Forty-eight hours of helping to deliver ice cream and other frozen desserts to restaurants, on a circular route that had taken in three countries and given very few opportunities for sleep, had taken every ounce of zest out of her.

She turned away from the lorry and, on the third attempt, hoisted her bag onto her shoulder and set off along the cypress-tree-lined path that led to the farmhouse.

Minty had spent every summer in Oschia since she'd turned seven and yet, on evenings like this, with the sunset beginning to turn the countryside red-gold, the landscape still had the power to make her stop and stare, drink it in. It was an idyllic setting.

The old stone house was positioned in the middle of a row of terraced plateaux that climbed down the hillside. At the top of the hill the small Oschian town clung on precariously. To one side she saw the medieval town walls gleaming gold in the evening sun, the tower of the medieval church jutting high above; in every other direction were a hundred different shades of green, as far as the eye could see.

It was only a couple of hundred yards down the driveway yet every weary step felt like a mile. Luckily the front door wasn't locked. Minty didn't think she was capable of finding her keys, hidden as they were somewhere amongst the tangle of essential toiletries, changes of underwear, sweet wrappers and other items she had considered necessary for her road trip. She turned the big wooden doorknob and almost fell into the large, marble-tiled hallway, dropping her bag with a relieved sigh.

'Honey, I'm home,' she called out, then sniffed. What was that smell? Onions, garlic, tomatoes, herbs, some kind of fish: the smell of a proper Italian kitchen. Her stomach rumbled painfully. It had been a while since the last food stop. At least that one had been over the Italian border; their journey through Austria, Slovenia and the tip of Germany had required more stop-offs at *bratwurst* stalls than Minty cared to remember.

The *currywurst* at the second one had definitely been a mistake; having two, an even bigger mistake.

Minty stayed in the hallway for a second, leaning against the panelled wall. Ahead was the staircase. All she had to do was somehow get herself up those stairs and she would be just one door away from her bed. Her gloriously comfortable bed with all the trimmings. What a beautiful contrast to the past two days, trying to nap squeezed into the front seat of the lorry between Gianno and Alfonso. Charming men, but not her sleeping companions of choice.

Minty swayed, torn between hunger and tiredness. Another enticing waft of garlic floated through the air and, with a regretful look up the stairs, Minty pulled herself together and went through the door to the kitchen to find the source of the heavenly smell.

The house was exactly the same as it had always been, unpretentious and homely with the large kitchen at its very heart. Taking up the whole back of the house, the combination kitchen, dining and family room was a warm, spacious area, the separate parts divided by a long tiled counter. On one side was the kitchen area, simple, with wooden doors and shelves, a marbled worktop and a huge range cooker. On the other a large table was set about with assorted, mismatched chairs. Further back, cosily clustered around the fireplace, were two old sofas. Floor-to-ceiling bookshelves covered one wall, filled with an assortment of battered, well-read Italian and English paperbacks, ancient board games and several incomplete packs of cards.

Minty had been raised in one of England's oldest and finest houses but she had never felt as at home there as she did here, had never loved it as much as she loved this room with its simple charm. Every piece of furniture had been lovingly chosen and pieced together. It was a much-loved home, far more appealing than the stunning, architecturally remodelled places she usually holidayed in.

Luca stood at the stove stirring the source of the heavenly smell with a spoon. At the sight of him Minty rocked back on her heels. There was something so inherently sexy about a handsome man cooking. It really wasn't fair; like a man holding a puppy or a baby, or taking his granny to church, the act added an extra glow, a sweetness to the sensuality.

He was dressed in snug-fitting, worn black jeans, in parts so faded they were grey, and a simple black T-shirt. The lack of colour should have been austere, especially teamed with his dark hair, but he looked good, the jeans showcasing long, powerful legs; the T-shirt skimming the smooth stomach; the short sleeves defining the muscles on his olive-skinned arms. Yep, he looked good, Minty thought dreamily.

She shook her head angrily, clearing the fog as best as she could. Goodness, she must be tired, standing here mooning over *Luca,* of all people! She was hungry, that was all; her brain was confusing the cook with the food.

'That smells delicious.'

Luca didn't bother to look round. 'Separate meals, remember?'

'I'll make the spaghetti,' she said as coaxingly as she could.

Luca spun round, horror on his face, tomato sauce splattering everywhere from the spoon he still held. '*Mio Dio*, do you still know nothing about food?' he said. "First of all this is *cioppino*—a soup. A simple salad and some ciabatta are all it needs. Secondly, if you think I would trust you with cooking pasta, you are delusional—unless at some point in the last six years you learned what *al dente* means, which I doubt very much. Thirdly, if it was a stew I would team it with something heartier than spaghetti: *farfalle* or maybe *bucatini*.' The amber eyes glazed over as he considered his options.

'I have done several cooking courses, you know,' Minty said, ignoring Luca's outburst. He couldn't help himself. Gio was just the same, convinced that nobody

could cook as well as he did, especially not someone unfortunate enough to be English. 'I can even *make* pasta,
not just cook it. How about I cut the bread?'

Luca's withering glare would have wilted a lesser
mortal. Luckily Minty was made of sterner stuff—and
had been weathering his glares for years. 'So it can go
stale? No, thank you.'

'Wash the salad? Or will I make the lettuce leaves
too wet? Be too rough with the cucumbers?'

Luca continued to stare for a few seconds longer then
shrugged, turning back to the stove to resume stirring.
Minty, taking silence for acquiescence, padded over
to the large American-style fridge and opened it, sur-
veying the huge array of contents. 'Only four types of
lettuce leaves; Luca, your standards are slipping,' she
said. Suddenly she felt far more awake, either from the
prospect of dinner or rediscovering the old joy of baiting
Luca. Or both. 'I'm not sure I can work with such ingredients,' she continued, throwing a provocative glance
over her shoulder. He was standing ramrod-straight,
radiating disapproval.

She removed the salad leaves, by the look of them
picked fresh that day, and carried them over to the sink
to wash. For a few minutes there was silence as they
worked side by side. Minty had never really cooked with
anyone else before. It was oddly comfortable.

'Can you pass the garlic?' she said after a while.

Luca eyed her suspiciously. 'Why?'

'Well, I could put it at the door and ward off vam-
pires, but I was thinking of making a vinaigrette for the
salad and to dip the bread into. Your call.'

The corners of Luca's mouth curled in a reluctant
smile and he tossed a small white bulb over to Minty,
who caught it one-handed with an elaborate flourish.

Standing there, knife in one hand, chopping board in front of her, no small talk, Minty was aware of an odd sensation.

She was almost content.

Dinner tasted as good as it smelt, helped, Minty was at pains to point out, by her perfectly seasoned vinaigrette. Afterwards, she collected the dishes and took them into the kitchen, waving Luca away when he came to help. 'Although I still think both my salad and the dressing were masterpieces,' she said, 'I do have to concede that you did the bulk of the cooking. It's only fair I clear up.'

Luca wasn't going to argue. He took his wine and a small plate of grapes and cheese over to the sofa and opened up his laptop, pulling up the spreadsheet Alessandro, his head of sales, had emailed over earlier that evening. He usually put at least an hour in after dinner; working from home sometimes gave things a different perspective.

Five minutes later it was as unread as when he had opened it. His eyes kept wandering over to Minty, who was industriously rinsing out pans. She looked tired; her hair was pulled back in a knot and she was still wearing the light trousers and simple knitted top she had put on two days ago when she had left to do the deliveries. But she hadn't come in complaining about how exhausted she was, how achy her limbs were—and he knew they would be, after two days in such a confined space.

It was almost impossible to work, to concentrate, with Minty so visible, so present. Since she had arrived she had kept her word and had stayed in her room at night, eaten separately and kept out of his way. They had barely seen each other to exchange a muttered greeting. Just as he wanted, as he had insisted.

And yet tonight he found himself moved by the weariness in her eyes. It was the same old story. He couldn't resist being her knight in shining armour, whether she wanted him to or not.

They might have spent most of their lives at loggerheads, but occasionally an unofficial, unacknowledged truce would be called. That first summer she'd come to stay, Luca had spent one memorable day playing old board games with the broken-hearted small girl after she'd discovered her father had chosen to go to St Tropez with his latest girlfriend instead of making a promised visit to Oschia.

Luca still had a fondness for Cluedo.

On her father's third wedding day—a small, intimate affair for around two hundred guests, including a celebrity magazine, but not the groom's only offspring—Luca had taken twelve-year-old Minty on an illicit road trip, pillioned on the back of his beloved Vespa. Rose had been furious when they had finally rocked back up long after dark, dirty, exhausted, exhilarated. Until she had seen the light shining in Minty's eyes.

At sixteen, Minty's boyfriend had dumped her by text. Another impromptu road trip, this time in Luca's teeny Fiat—a present from Gio and Rose, who'd shared a fear of very young men driving powerful cars. Not that Luca had ever been likely to drive recklessly, not after his parents' accident. They had headed south and ended up in Rome for an afternoon of sightseeing, shopping and very expensive coffee.

The last truce of all had been the night after Rose's funeral. Luca's hands tightened on the laptop keyboard at the memory. Six years later and he could still taste Minty, still recall exactly how it had felt to run his hands down those long, long legs; up over that supple

waist to the swell of her small, firm breasts; her gasps
and murmured endearments, begging him please not
to stop, never to stop. He stared sightlessly at his keyboard, willing the memory to fade.

For the aftermath of these truces was always the
same: distance; disdain. Minty acting out worse than
usual, as if to wipe out those rare moments of vulnerability. And that last time she'd simply disappeared. For
six years Luca hadn't known who to despise more—
himself for taking advantage of a grieving girl not yet
out of her teens, or Minty for running away.

And now she was back. Wiping dishes in his kitchen
as if they really were the family she had refused to
allow them to be.

She was surprising him. There had been no moan-
ing, no trying to shirk the long, arduous schedule he had
put together for her. It was still early days, less than a
week since she had taken up the challenge, but he had
ensured her every moment was filled: a 4:00 a.m. start
day for the morning milking; a gruelling day in the
frozen-food section of the warehouse followed by two
days on the road. Tomorrow would be spent in one of
the kitchens; the weekend would be serving in the café
which sold Di Tore Dolce products directly to the public.

'I love that you haven't changed anything,' she said,
banging the dishwasher door shut. She picked up a cloth
and began to wipe down the sides. 'The same dishes,
pans, worktops. I like that it's all the same.'

Luca put the laptop down on the table in front of him
and leant back, the glass of wine in his hand. 'What
would I have changed?' he asked.

Minty shrugged. 'Sleek, black leather sofas and
chrome everywhere,' she suggested. 'Knocking through
into the next room. Creating an outdoor kitchen.'

Luca shuddered, looking round at the comfortable, cosy room. 'That sounds completely horrible.'

'Standard young CEO fare,' she said. 'The shinier, bigger and more expensive, the better. Hugely overcompensating, of course.' She winked at him. 'Good to see a man comfortable with what he has.'

'This is part of my family's history,' Luca said, ignoring the wink *and* the innuendo. 'Furniture made and chosen by my parents and grandparents. By Rose. Why would I change it?'

'I'm glad you didn't.' Minty wrung out the cloth and hung it up over the sink taps before collecting her wine glass and bag and bringing them over to the sofas. Luca was relieved when she chose the other one to curl up into, her long legs folded under her. 'There are so many old houses like this that have been remodelled. Botox for houses, turning them into wrinkle-free, soulless show-homes. This place wears its history proudly, wrinkles and all.'

Luca twirled the wine glass round a couple of times, as if looking for answers in the ruby depths. It hadn't even occurred to him to change the house, to modernise it, although all around the local area houses like this one were being done up, turned into holiday homes or country retreats. 'I'm not a big fan of leather and chrome,' he said. 'I guess I always imagined my children being raised in the same house that I was, eating at the same table, off the same plates. I always thought a house like this should be filled with children. It seems too big for just one.'

'There were two of us in the holidays,' Minty reminded him.

'*Si*, but you were never a childlike child. Always so

knowing, so old for your years. When you weren't doing something crazy, that is.'

Minty had raised her glass ready to take a sip but at his words she set it back down on the table. 'I wasn't the only one. Old for my years, I mean, not crazy.' She laughed. 'Did you *ever* misbehave, Luca?'

He shook his head, smiling. 'Only when you were with me.'

Their eyes met, blue held by gold, sudden awareness blazing between them, remembering the last time they had misbehaved together here in this room, on the very sofa Minty was curled up on. Awareness that it would be so easy for him to put down his glass and move just a few steps over to her. Awareness that it would take just one touch, that all he needed to do was run one finger down her cheek to the corner of her mouth, onto those full lips.

He swallowed, hard. It was tempting, when she looked at him like that: guileless, teasing, daring. Vulnerable.

But the price was too high to pay. It had always been too high.

None of her emotions were real. It was all a game.

He looked away, deliberately breaking the invisible line of attraction linking them. He took a sip of wine and leant back, to all appearances relaxed.

Even if he was coiled tighter than a snake in winter.

'So, how many children would it take to fill this house?' If Minty was affected by the sudden attraction—or by Luca's withdrawal—she wasn't showing it.

It was frustrating. But safer.

'Four.'

She spluttered. 'Four? That's ambitious.'

Luca eyed her coolly. 'I am ambitious. In every area of my life.'

'Obviously. You're, what, twenty-nine now? Better get a move on if you want to make it to number four. Unless you're hoping for one a year?'

He shook his head, smiling. 'Not quite that fast, but I would like them sooner rather than later.'

'So who's the lucky brood mare?' When Luca didn't reply, Minty raised an eyebrow. 'You're not planning single fatherhood, are you?'

'I hoped to be married with at least one child by now, but it didn't work out. I was engaged,' he offered, surprising himself with his openness.

'What happened?'

He shrugged. 'We wanted different things.'

Minty smiled, although it didn't reach her eyes, which were dark with sympathy. 'Welcome to the club. You'll have to do better than one failed engagement if you want premier membership, though.'

'Thanks; I'll stick to the basic category.'

She sipped her wine pensively then slid him a look from under those long eyelashes. 'So who was it? Do I know her?'

'Francesca Di Rossi.'

Amusement flared on the mobile face. 'So she did it. Well done, Francesca. Lucky escape, if you ask me.'

Luca wasn't sure what reaction, if any, he'd expected. The dark amusement in Minty's voice was not it.

'So she did it,' Luca repeated slowly. 'What do you mean by that?' Although he suspected he knew what her answer would be.

'You must know you were considered quite the catch locally: tall, dark, not too horrid to look at. Add in your family connections and the fact you employ half the district... I'm surprised prospective replacements aren't queuing up around the block. Although the "four children" may be putting less committed candidates off.'

'It's not something I advertise.' But her words were still rankling him. 'Why "lucky escape"?'

Minty shrugged. 'I just wouldn't have thought you and Francesca were very compatible, that's all. I didn't know her very well, but I know her type. I bet she would have remodelled the house before you got round to cutting the wedding cake.'

Luca blinked in surprise. Francesca *had* been full of suggestions: new bathrooms; a new kitchen. He had thought at first she was simply taking an interest in his life. The truth was she had wanted to change his life. Change Luca.

'I thought she loved it round here, wanted to stay, settle down.' Luca couldn't believe he was volunteering the information. After they'd split up he had shut the door on that part of his past and had barely given Francesca a second thought.

Unlike Minty. How could one interrupted night have made more of an impression than two years with Francesca?

'She didn't?' Minty's voice jolted him out of his thoughts.

'Not at all. She thought I should move the office part of the business to Florence so I could be near that side of my family.' His mouth twisted wryly. 'Near the aristocratic side. Turned out Francesca was a big fan of titles. She wanted us to have a fancy apartment and spend our time in fancy restaurants with fancy people. I wanted to stay here.'

'You couldn't compromise? Some time here, some time there?'

Luca shook his head. The truth was he hadn't even considered it. 'Honestly? I don't think either of us cared enough deep down to make it work. For me, my work is here; my life. But Francesca felt stifled here. How do you compromise on that? In the end she found someone who wanted the same things she did. They're very happy and that's great.' It was. When Luca analysed his feelings around Francesca's infidelity, he felt a little humiliation—and a much greater relief.

Minty nodded sagely. 'She was your starter fiancée—much better than a starter marriage, in my opinion.'

'*Che?*'

She settled back, stretching slightly, and despite himself his eyes were drawn to the way her top stretched up, the enticing flash of midriff. 'I bet you thought settling down was the right thing to do. There she was, a local girl. She knew the right people, went to the right parties, said the right things, was there when you needed her. Am I right?'

How on earth did she know that? Luca's face must have shown his amazement, as Minty laughed. 'I told you, I know girls like her. I've *been* a girl like her. Far better to find out you're incompatible now than in ten years' time when you have children. If you ask me, that mother of your four offspring won't be someone quite so obvious. Someone who doesn't make it quite so easy at the beginning, but who is comfortable to be with at the end.'

'What made you so wise?' The perception surprised him. Luca had never doubted that Minty had layers; he just didn't think she had depth.

'Three fiancés.' She laughed as she said it but there was a glimmer of pain in her eyes that even Minty's best carefree expression couldn't hide. 'I am the starter-fiancé expert.'

'In that case, your theory doesn't work,' Luca said. 'Shouldn't there be one starter, not an entire buffet of them?'

'Oh, they weren't *my* starter fiancés,' Minty said. 'I was theirs. I'm the mistake that showed them exactly what they don't want in a future partner. It's a gift, really. I should get some kind of humanitarian award for it.'

Luca hated it when she did this: showed a hint of her inner self and covered it up with a brave face and a few self-deprecating jokes. It made a man want to get up and walk over to where she sat, supremely grace-ful, head up, eyes glittering, daring the world to feel sorry for her. It made a man want to gather her into his arms, pull her close and tell her it was all right, that she didn't have to pretend.

It made a man remember just how yielding and vul-nerable she could really be. Made a man think of hard kisses, soft caresses; how a man could get lost in those lips, those eyes. In her promise. He'd come so close to getting lost.

But he'd come to his senses.

It still sickened him, how close he had come to tak-ing advantage of her, of her youth, of her grief. The only saving grace was that he had stopped, pushed her away, before it was too late.

By the time he'd risen from his sleepless, guilt-ridden bed, before he could apologise, make things right, she had gone, snuck away in the night.

Straight back to England. To Barty. To her boy-lover.

Luca looked over at Minty, her long legs curled under her, her head high despite the deep shadows under her eyes, despite the lingering sadness in their blue depths. A small part of him—the part of him that didn't want a five-year plan; that didn't want a predictable path; the ruthlessly suppressed part of him that occasionally, just occasionally wished to be spontaneous—wanted to walk over, raise her to her feet and pull her in close. But no. He couldn't take the risk; he couldn't trust her no matter how much she seemed to have changed.

Slowly, deliberately, he got to his feet. 'Maybe you're right,' he said as lightly as he could. 'Better a failed engagement than a bad marriage. And I learnt a lot from Francesca. Compatibility, shared goals, they're what's important in life; that's what I'm looking for. A woman who values family, a home, a quiet life.'

'Apron optional?'

Her eyebrows were raised enquiringly, a suspiciously innocent look on her face. Luca suppressed a smile. She wasn't going to get to him that easily. 'Would I like to come home to the smell of freshly baked bread whilst my bathed *bambinos* cluster about me? Of course. I think any man or woman would. But no, I am not looking for a homemaker, unless that's what she wants, of course. I'm looking for someone I can rely on. Someone who relies on me. A partnership. Someone who will be there when I wake up.'

And on that parting shot he left the room, all too aware that he had yet another sleepless night ahead of him. Another night hyper-aware of his maddening guest so near, so far.

But he didn't look back.

CHAPTER FOUR

'I'M IN HEAVEN; actual, real-life heaven.' Minty looked about, barely restraining herself from clapping her hands in delight. It was a child's dream. Actually, Minty corrected herself, it was anyone in possession of working taste buds' dream. A long, long counter was filled with box after box of brightly coloured *gelato*. Another one was stacked high with mouth-watering cakes and pastries. A few tables and chairs were dotted about inside and the full-length patio doors were flung open to the seating area outside.

'So, this area is open to the public,' Natalia explained as she took Minty through the exhaustive menu. 'Take away or eat in, by the portion or the box. It's on all the tourist maps so we get a great deal of passing trade, plus potential trade customers who like to drop in casually—and the odd competitor snooping around as well.'

The café had been opened at some point in the past six years, another of Luca's innovations. The place was full of them. And the staff loved it. It was like working with a living saint, Minty thought. The wonderful Signor Di Tore—or Signor Luca to the older staff, who remembered every visit the infant prodigy had paid to the factory and could happily recount them in mind-numbing detail. His every word was listened to adoringly, every pronouncement admired, every movement scrutinised.

No wonder he was insufferable.

'You have got the hang of it very quickly,' Natalia said admiringly as Minty deftly dealt with a large group of teenagers, each with a different and complicated request. 'You're a natural.'

'Not really,' Minty confessed. 'I ran a café back in London. Cupcakes; they're pretty big there right now.' She sighed. Her father's manager was keeping an eye on them while she was exiled from the family fold. She hoped he wouldn't interfere too much, or try to enforce his tastes on the staff. His favourite pudding was spotted dick. Minty shuddered. Even her talented bakers would have a hard time creating a tasty treat with that as an inspiration.

A range of cakes based on other traditional English classics might work, though. Minty mechanically served the next couple as her mind went through some ideas. Sticky toffee pudding, jam roly-poly and custard, rhubarb crumble, apple pie—all the basis of perfect little cupcakes. She might be banned from setting foot on the premises but her father couldn't stop her from texting her ideas through. 'Old school', they could call the range. A vanilla sponge, rhubarb middle topped with a smidge of *crème anglaise* and finished off with a buttery crumble: perfect for the autumn. Mini summer puddings sandwiched together with cream for the coming season. Possibly some variations on a scone?

She rinsed out the metal scoop, her mind still humming with ideas, and pushed it firmly into the *frutti di bosco,* scraping out a perfect round scoop and placing it carefully into the paper cup. The gelato was a deep purple, bursting with berries. As she handed over the cup to an eagerly outstretched hand, a glimmer of an idea began to grow insistently.

As the post-lunch siesta hour kicked in, the flow of customers quietened down and for the first time in several hours there was no one waiting to be served. It was nice to have a few moments alone with her thoughts. The few customers that were left were content to sit out in the sun sipping their drinks. Natalia had taken advantage of the lull to slip out for some lunch.

Minty took out the small notepad and pencil she'd been issued with and began to sketch out some ideas. Keeping busy kept her mind away from dangerous topics, pushing memories of the other night with Luca firmly out of her mind. It was just that there'd been a moment, a few moments, when Luca had looked at her as if he'd seen something more. As if she weren't just a thorn in his side, not just a spoilt child.

He'd looked at her like that before. Another memory she'd tried to forget.

Memories could be inconvenient. It was so easy to make them selective. They focussed on molten eyes, on heat, on want. They forgot the burning chill of rejection. They forgot how it felt to lie on a sofa suddenly impossibly alone, skirt rucked up, shirt undone, lips open with need. They forgot the look of horror. Of guilt. Of rejection.

They said you never forgot your first time. It was as true of rejection as it was of anything else.

But memories could also make you hope. Far better to forget, to live in the here and now.

'You look quite at home there.' Minty jumped at the familiar voice. He was like the devil: think of him and he appeared. She looked across to see him standing at one of the open doors, leaning against the frame, laughter in his eyes as he looked her up and down.

Another day, another outfit so uncharacteristic she defied any paparazzo to recognise her in it. The white, button-up dress was almost clinical in its severity; her hair was smoothed back, covered with a small pink scarf. She gave him a twirl. 'What do you think?'

'You certainly look the part,' he agreed. 'Having fun?'

'It's not all new to me, you know,' she said. Why did he always seem to be laughing at her? 'I do own three cafés and, contrary to popular belief, I have actually worked in them.'

Luca raised a sceptical brow as he sauntered into the café, weekend casual in faded blue jeans and a bright-blue short-sleeved shirt. Minty wanted to wipe that scepticism off his face, see it replaced with respect. After six solid days of work, she deserved some respect. 'The first one, I set up from scratch: painted the walls, chose the recipes, mixed cake batter until all I could smell was sugar and egg and butter. Stood behind a counter and smiled as people spent ten minutes choosing which one they wanted.'

'So why aren't you there now?'

Now, that was a good question. Unfortunately Minty didn't have a good answer. 'I told you, they are part of my trust fund, so therefore forbidden,' she said. Honesty compelled her to carry on. 'Daddy said as I had barely set foot inside them in months I couldn't claim that I was needed there, that they were doing all right without me. I guess he was right.'

He didn't say anything, just wandered round the counter and came to stand next to her, a disturbingly comfortable presence. Calmly, without any fuss or fanfare, he began to make a couple of coffees, loading up a tray with a few small savouries and a helping of the delicious-looking salad they used as garnish. 'You must be starving,' he said finally. 'Come, sit down. If anyone comes in I'll take over.'

Minty considered arguing, asserting her independence, pointing out that Natalia wouldn't be long and she could easily wait. But, without quite knowing how, she found herself following him over to a quiet corner with a view of the counter.

'It's not that I was lazy,' she said suddenly, standing beside the table as he pulled out a chair. He glanced at her, eyes mildly enquiring, no judgement on his face. Minty sank into the chair and pulled the plate over, picking up one of the tiny, perfect pastries and turning it round in her fingers, her appetite gone.

'Joe thought they gave out the wrong message—elitist establishments in expensive areas charging exorbitant prices. Not at all compatible with his values. He preferred that I spent my time volunteering or helping him. So, I did.'

She didn't know why it was so important that Luca understood, that he didn't think badly of her—at least, any more badly than he already did. But it did matter.

'Okay, that's what Joe wanted. What did you want?' It was said so gently it almost hurt her. There had been too many times in the past when the only person who had shown a glimmer of understanding was Luca.

She had usually punished him for it.

She continued to twist the mini focaccia between her fingers. The bread was dissolving into a mass of crumbs, the aubergine and mozzarella filling sliding out onto the plate below, releasing an aroma of onions,

garlic and oregano. She stared at the mess she was creating, searching for answers. What did she want?

It was the million-dollar question. And she had no
idea.

She quite liked it here. Quite liked today, keeping
busy, being useful, good at what she did even if it was
just serving ice cream. And the other night, the meal,
the company—she'd enjoyed that just a little too much.

Until he had shut her out and walked away. Again.

Minty raised her head and smiled across at Luca. He
was still looking at her intently, concern etched on his
handsome features. The sudden urge to sink onto him,
into him, to allow him to shoulder her burdens was im-
mense, almost irresistible.

'I think I want to live life on the wild side,' she said.
'Have my *gelato* before my savoury. But I can't decide
whether to go with the fruit, the chocolate or the really
decadent creamy flavours. What do you recommend?'

Luca was doing his best to forget about Minty. He
stayed late at the office, eating dinner there or calling
in at a local restaurant on the way home. Most days
this week he had only seen his unwanted house guest
in the mornings. She was usually just wandering into
the kitchen as he left for work.

It didn't mean he wasn't aware of her.

At home he was haunted by the scent of lemons that
seemed to have permeated every inch of his house,
somehow even his own pillows and sheets. He woke
up inhaling the fresh, spicy scent and found himself
unable to get back to sleep, knowing that she was just
a few metres away.

Her stuff was everywhere. It wasn't that she was
untidy; she wasn't, particularly, but she did have an in-

nate gift of taking over a space and making it her own. Her fruit and yogurt concoctions were in his fridge, her magazines on his table, her cardigan hung over the back of his chair, her shoes by his door. The only places that were safe from the slow but steady encroachment were his bedroom and bathroom.

Apart from the scent of lemons.

And it was worse at work.

Everybody loved her. In less than two weeks she had learnt the names of not just every member of staff, but the names of their husbands, wives, children, grandchildren, dogs, rabbits and goldfish. Wherever she went, people greeted her, stopped her. If she wasn't discussing haircuts with Bella on reception, she was asking Mario about how his dog's operation had gone or was admiring pictures of Maria's newest grandchild.

Luca thought of himself as a hands-on, informal, friendly boss; he had known some of these people all his life. Yet Minty had discovered more about their lives, their worries, their joys, in days than he had in all that time.

Her ex was wrong, he thought. She would have made an excellent politician's wife.

Even in the privacy of his office her name was brought up constantly. Everyone was delighted with her hard work, her enthusiasm, her attempts to speak Italian and her ideas. The staff of Di Tore Dolce were rapidly becoming fully paid-up members of the Minty Davenport fan club.

'Luca!' And here she was: in his thoughts, his dreams, his conversations, his home. And now in his office.

'*Buongiorno.*' He didn't mean to sound so formal, so aloof, every time he spoke to her.

It just seemed safer. Twice she had got to him. Twice he had broken his resolve to keep clear, remember that she was unsafe, toxic.

Not that she seemed to notice. She was practically shaking with excitement as she danced up to his desk, a small paper cup in her hand.

'Look what I did!' She put the cup down on his desk and took a step backwards, beaming like a proud mother hen. 'All by myself. Well, actually, with huge amounts of help and input and advice and supervision, but *practically* all by myself.'

Luca gave up. It was impossible to maintain a formal distance in the face of such all-consuming enthusiasm. 'What is it?' He peered into the cup. 'It looks like *gelato.*'

'Of course it's *gelato*! You own a *gelato* factory, you noodle. What was I going to make, some sort of new dog food?'

With a smile, he conceded the point.

'But this is my very own recipe, mixed by my very own hands. It's for the autumn special-editions. Tomas said to let you try it. That's good, right? It means it's passed the first test?' She bit down on her lower lip with suppressed excitement, drawing his attention to its fullness. 'Do you want me to tell you what it is?'

Luca dragged his eyes away from her sparkling eyes and the sensual curve of her mouth. They were too distracting.

'No, no, I'll try it first.'

She was jigging from foot to foot in her excitement. 'Go on, then!'

Some men were wine snobs, closing their eyes and inhaling before tasting. Luca enjoyed a fine wine but didn't take it too seriously. After all, any local vineyard sold a decent table wine for just a few euros. *Gelato*, however; well, *gelato* he took very seriously, especially if it had his name on it.

He pulled the paper cup close, took the small tasting spoon and scooped a mouthful out of the cup, examining it closely. It was a pale, creamy colour, flecked with small biscuit-coloured chunks and a streak of clear fruit puree. Cautiously, he held it close to his nose and took a deep breath. Ah... Apple and cinnamon were the most pervasive flavours, instantly filling his nostrils with the scent of home baking, country kitchens. Autumn smells. He nodded slowly. So far, so good.

He brought the spoon to his mouth and carefully licked just a small portion of the ice cream, rolling the cold, creamy morsel round his mouth until he had savoured every flavour. The *gelato* base was creamier than usual; he would guess it had been made with a vanilla *crème anglaise* then swirled through with the apple puree and cinnamon. And the chunks...

He slid the rest of the portion off the spoon and into his mouth: a soft, crumbly, sweet texture. Sponge; apple, cinnamon, custard and sponge. It was delicious.

'Well? What do you think?'

'Very good indeed.'

'Isn't it? It came to me at the weekend, when I was working in the café. At first I was thinking of cupcakes but then I thought about the expansion and a way to corner the UK market. What better than English classic puds with an Italian *gelato* twist? Eve's pudding— which is this one—crumbles, pies, even arctic roll? Of course,' she added, 'I might steal my own idea for cupcakes too. There's no direct competition. Arctic roll cupcakes might be rather fun.'

Minty had perched on his desk, one long leg slung

across the other, and her words were almost drowned out by the roaring in his ears. *Mio Dio*, did she have any idea of the effect she was having on him, sitting so close?

Today her formal office wear had been discarded and she was wearing a pretty summer dress in a deep sky-blue reminiscent of her eyes. Her legs were bare and far too close. Within touching distance. Her feet were clad in flimsy velvet flip-flops, her toenails painted to match her dress.

He really should say something about inappropriate footwear but all the breath had been sucked out of his chest.

Oblivious, she rattled on. 'For all our sophistication, we are traditionalists at heart, especially with pudding. If you are going for a soft opening in the autumn, then this kind of stodgy comfort food might be the way forward.'

He could just put his hand out and touch her thigh, run his hand along those long, toned legs. Or put both hands on her waist and swivel her around. Pull her close to the end of the desk, down onto his lap, facing him.

Dear God, his mouth was dry. He stood up abruptly and skirted past her to the other end of the office, to the safety of his water cooler, to the safety of distance.

Luca took a sip of the ice-cold water, and then another, eyes focussed on the painting on the opposite wall, a vibrant abstract of the local countryside. But he wasn't noticing the colours, the skilful brushstrokes, the stunning overall effect. He was trying to dampen down this sudden, fierce wave of desire that had swamped him.

What was wrong with him? So she had nice legs. So did hundreds of other women and he didn't find himself wanting to stroke their thighs, thank goodness. That kind of behaviour could get a man into serious trouble.

Blonde hair didn't usually do it for him, either. That one night with Minty aside, his previous relationships had all been with brunettes.

Grimly he began to recite in his head all the reasons walking over to her and pulling her close were such a bad idea: she was working for him, she was practically family and she was a city girl with a life she was going to return to very, very soon.

The last time he'd given in to an urge to kiss her it had not ended well.

And, he told himself firmly, they had nothing in common. Oh, she was filled with excitement and passion for his business right now. That was because it was new and fun, different.

They both knew she wasn't going to stick around.

But, a little insistent voice in his head pointed out, what did all that matter? Sure, Luca wanted a wife, a family, but it wasn't as if he was dating anybody right now. Was he planning to live like a monk until he found the perfect candidate? Minty wasn't actually working for him, she was playing at working. He wasn't her boss; she could walk away any time.

She was no longer a girl. There was nothing wrong in wanting her now.

And she wanted him too. He'd seen it in those deep blue eyes as mysterious as the sea. He'd seen it in the flush of her cheeks, the curve of her lips. If he walked over there now and kissed her, she would respond. He knew that at some primeval level with utter certainty.

He just had to push that knowledge away. Far, far away.

'So, next I'm spending some time in packaging and design and Tomas suggested that if you like the ice cream

I could concentrate on the packaging for it. Not just for this, but for the concept. That's if I'm staying. The two weeks are nearly up, after all.'

Of course she had won; she knew it. There was no reason to fail her. A new start, a challenge, a wager: she thrived on all these things.

And it had been fun. Unexpectedly fun.

Working with people all day, all part of a team, all trying to attain the same goal, was a buzz. Why did people say the nine-to-five was dull? It was absolutely stimulating. Of course, she conceded, she wasn't having the full experience, moving from department to department as she was, but she had never felt so full of ideas, of creativity. Even at night she lay there with ideas buzzing round her brain, unable to sleep with it all.

Okay, it wasn't just the work stopping her sleeping. Sharing a house with Luca was a serious mistake. Just knowing she could slip out of her bed, pad along the corridor to his room and slip in beside him was torture.

But what if he said no? He had refused her before. He wanted a woman to have his babies, all four of them. He didn't want a ditzy debutante who fluttered from project to project, fiancé to fiancé, like a pollen-drunk butterfly. He wanted a sensible woman in sensible shoes with a sensible attitude.

And thank goodness he did, she told herself sternly. It was too risky. This one would hurt—had hurt. She might not bounce back this time.

If she was staying, she should seriously consider finding her own place well away from temptation. Maybe the local convent had a room. 'So?'

'So?' he echoed.

'Have I passed? Do I get to stay?'

'If you want to.' He sounded indifferent, as if her

arrangements, her presence here, meant nothing to him. Perhaps it didn't. Why should it? Occasionally she thought he felt it too, that he *might* be attracted to her. But attraction meant nothing without respect. Good genes had given her a healthy metabolism, body and bone structure. Money and an abundance of leisure time had allowed her to enhance those genetic gifts. Minty was under no illusions: a toned body, good skin and thick hair were nice to have. But she hoped she was worth more than their sum.

She hoped she'd have the chance to find out how *much* more one day. Being here, working with people who didn't seem to care that her father was an earl, her mother an actress, or didn't care that she had been tabloid fodder since her wild-child teens, people who only expected hard work, was liberating. It gave her hope.

'Of course I want to stay.'

'Of course,' he murmured. 'Of course, why would you want the financial freedom selling your shares to me would give you? Of course you would prefer to get up early every day and work for nine hours, five days a week.'

'That's how most people live.'

'Yes, but *you* are not most people.' Minty flinched at the sardonic gleam in his eyes, another reason not to get too close. He'd always had a disconcerting habit of seeing more than she revealed, seeing past her armour. 'However, if you wish to stay I will, of course, honour our agreement. Unless...' He paused reflectively. The amber eyes blazed; he looked at his most devilish. 'Can you handle a new deal?'

He sounded so calm, so superior. Minty was tempted to say no, to flounce out, head held high. They'd made a deal and she had won. He couldn't take that away from her.

But she was intrigued. Damn those gaming ancestors of hers.

'Okay,' she said. 'I'll consider what you have to say.'

'You can stay. I can see you would be useful in the marketing department working on the English-language campaigns. You *have* worked hard the past two weeks. Everyone is full of praise—and it's what Rose would have wanted—so, we'll sort out a job description, salary; everything will be done properly. And, of course, I expect you to take up your seat on the board. But when you get bored...' He looked her straight in the eyes. 'And you will get bored, Minty, we both know that— probably sooner rather than later. Then you sell your shares and you don't come near my company again. *Capisce?*'

Oh, he was good, too good; too damn perceptive.

She slid off the desk, pulling her dress down as she did so. 'What if I have a genuine reason?' she asked sweetly. 'A new job, a baby, a fiancé who sticks around, a broken leg, an emergency back home? What if I work for you for ten years and get a new opportunity? Does that still count?'

He laughed, a genuine burst of humour that surprised her, made her smile with the infectiousness of it. 'If you are here in ten years I'll...' He cast about for an appropriate expression.

'In English, we say "eat my hat",' Minty informed him helpfully and smiled back over at him. The smile wavered on her lips. Luca was looking at her intently, the humour disappearing as suddenly as it had arrived, an unreadable expression in his amber eyes. The contrast with his olive skin and those long, dark lashes was startling; it made him seem wild, almost wolflike. They were eyes a girl could get lost in, eyes that could make you forget where you were, what you were doing.

She swayed, taking a tiny step closer, and then another, hypnotised by those eyes, by the heat she could see burning in them, when the shrill sound of her phone's ringtone blared out. She looked about for her phone, desperate to shut the intrusive noise off, to get back to the intimacy that had suddenly flared up. The noise was coming from her bag which was slumped on the desk behind her, next to the rapidly melting ice cream.

The ice cream wasn't the only thing melting in the suddenly stuffy room.

Her legs like jelly, Minty wobbled to the desk, reaching out to grasp it for support. This wasn't right. Luca hadn't even touched her! How could a look, one look, affect her this way? She fumbled for her phone, but by the time she had pulled it out it was too late; the call had diverted to voicemail.

She took a deep breath. She was going to say something. She just wasn't sure what. *'Don't look at me that way.'* Or maybe, *'Kiss me.'*

Possibly both.

She turned round, the words trembling on her lips. But Luca was gone.

CHAPTER FIVE

'GOOD MORNING.'

Cheerful, well-modulated tones rang clearly across the room. The tones of someone who embraced each morning, someone raised on kippers, kidneys and anaemic toast. Someone raised on hearty pre-breakfast tramps across fields and woodland trails, a well-trained spaniel at their heel.

'I hope you slept well?' the cheerful inquisition continued.

'Buongiorno.' Forcing a polite smile on his face, Luca turned to face her. He might prefer silence, a brisk walk, black coffee and a newspaper to help him wake up properly but Minty was a member of that despised breed: breakfast chatterer.

And, annoyingly, using his newspaper as a barrier wasn't working. She just chatted on regardless. He lowered it reluctantly. He should have gone in earlier, had his coffee and read his paper in the peaceful privacy of his office.

She was dressed and ready to go, a file by her side and the ubiquitous iPad in her hand. Sure, the effect looked industrious but Luca would bet good money that she was checking her social media accounts, not actually working. His mouth twisted wryly as he observed her. At least Minty was taking her new job seriously, sartorially at least, he noted. She definitely looked the part of a young marketing executive in a pretty grey dress that fell to just above the knee, teamed with a lemon cardigan and yet another flimsy pair of flip-flops, these the same colour as her cardigan. She had twisted her hair up into a knot with just a few tendrils hanging down. She looked as fresh as a lemon sorbet.

And just as desirable.

No, he reminded himself. *Don't go there.* But he felt that increasingly familiar pull towards her, the heating of his blood as it flowed through his veins. Minty by comparison looked as cool as the sorbet she resembled, sitting on the tiled counter as she swiped the tablet's screen, swinging those long, bare legs; slim, muscular, formed on the hockey fields of England's best schools.

He forced himself to look away, to concentrate on the coffee and paper before him, but his gaze was inexorably drawn to the lithe figure. Did she know how much it annoyed him when she did that? Counters were for chopping things on, for cooking, preparing, not for sitting. Not for swinging ridiculously long legs. Why didn't she sit in a chair like every other human being?

'I need to leave; do you want a lift?'

Okay, that was a little abrupt, but she didn't look surprised. She bit her bottom lip thoughtfully and drew his unwilling attention to the curve of her mouth and the full bottom lip that he knew was put to good use, charming its owner's way through life.

'A lift? Careful, Luca, a girl might think you enjoyed having her around.'

'It seems silly to be using two cars, that's all. Wasteful.'

Truth was, it was nice to have someone else around. The farmhouse was too big for one. It was crying out for conversation; music; laughter; love; noisy family suppers around the table.

And so was he.

'Thank you,' she said. 'A lift would be nice.' She sighed. 'I do appreciate you putting up with me. I'm sure you can't wait for me to be gone. I'll look for a room soon, but I'm not sure I can afford a house round here; I'll have to share.' She pulled a face. 'I'm sure Daddy will say it's good for me, but I don't see how rows about who ate the last yoghurt and whose turn it is to do the washing up are character-forming.'

'Don't rush. Take your time, save up a bit.' He saw the surprise in her eyes and elaborated, 'This was your home too, once. Rose would be glad that you are here.'

'Actually, it was always your home,' she corrected him gently. 'It couldn't have been easy, having your aunt and uncle move into your parents' house. And then for me to turn up as well; talk about salt in wounds.'

For one moment it was as if all the breath had been sucked out of his body and all Luca could do was stare at Minty. In all the years he had known her, she had never once acknowledged that he had a right to resent her presence. Maybe she was growing up after all, developing empathy. Becoming the woman he had always thought she could be.

He hoped not. That could complicate everything.

'I was grateful that Gio and Rose gave up their lives to move here so that I could have some continuity,' he said after the silence had stretched thin between them. 'The thought of moving to London after everything— leaving Italy, the countryside, my home, the factory, all my memories… I don't know if I would have coped. But I didn't have to. They moved here, took over the house and the business, raised me and allowed me to carry on. Your presence for a couple of months a year was a small price to pay.'

Minty laughed. 'You and I both know that isn't true; I was a royal pain in the butt. I resented you, you know. Rose was *my* aunt, the only person I really trusted, and suddenly she was miles away in a different country looking after you full time. I was so jealous.'

'It was a long time ago.' Luca suddenly knew two things with utter certainty: that he would have no peace whilst Minty was still in the house; and that he didn't want her to go. Not yet. 'Honestly, Minty. Stay. I'd like you to.'

Her eyes were filled with uncertainty as she stared at him, visibly considering her options, her face un- usually open, a mixture of hope and fear. Finally her troubled expression cleared and she nodded, relaxed. 'Thank you, Luca. I'd like that.'

'Good.' A weight slipped off his shoulders at her agreement, a weight he hadn't even known he was carrying. He had been alone too long. And, although Minty might not be the most restful of housemates, she was at least familiar. She had watched him grow from a sad, taciturn boy through to conscientious adolescence.

In a way, she was family.

He shrugged off that troubling thought. 'I just need to change, so I'll be leaving in about fifteen minutes; is that okay with you?'

'No problem, I'm ready to go when you are. I'll grab another coffee and a brioche and read my emails. Just yell when you're ready.'

Luca nodded and turned to go upstairs. He needed to change into his suit from his usual morning attire of comfy jeans and an old T-shirt. Whenever he had time he liked to get up early and go for a walk over some of the estate before coffee and the paper. One day he would have a dog to take with him—when he had a wife and a family—something big enough to take on long, country walks but not too overwhelming for small children. A spaniel, maybe, or an Italian greyhound.

One day...

'Oh!' Minty made a small muffled sound of pain. Luca turned quickly, expecting to see a spilt cup of coffee. Instead Minty was bolt upright, staring at her iPad screen, a haunted, betrayed look in her huge eyes, her mouth twisted as she swallowed back tears.

'What is it?' Luca was by her side in a flash, pulling the tablet from her unresisting fingers. Two pictures filled the screen. One was of Minty, a glass of wine in her hand, laughing, eyes glittering, wearing something that even in the photo looked expensive and short. His eyes skirted quickly over the close-up of generous cleavage and acres of thigh. The other was a photo of a young man, suited, hair neatly parted, holding hands with an equally sober-looking woman, her hair neatly pinned back. *Minty's Curse Strikes Again!* screamed the headline.

> *Three-times-unlucky socialite Lady Araminta Davenport is reeling from the news that ex-fiancé number three has announced his engagement to fellow politician Clara Church—less than three months since the dramatic collapse of his engagement to Minty.*
>
> *The blonde beauty, daughter of the Earl of Holgate and actress Coco Waters, has managed to bag a rock for her finger on three occasions—but has yet to make it down the aisle. Instead, each of*

*her fiancés has married another within six months
of breaking up with the former wild child.*

*'Minty's devastated,' said a close friend. 'She
wonders if it will ever be her turn.'*
*Who next for Lady Min? We've compiled a list of
the hottest possibilities. The lucky lady has already bagged a viscount, a rock star and a rising
politician! Who will she choose next time—and
will this one stick around?*

Underneath the article were headshots of several
young men the newspaper had thoughtfully collated
for her, ranging from minor European royalty to an
Eton-educated Shakespearian actor.

Minty glanced at the pictures over Luca's shoulder.
'That's the best they can do? At least two of these men
are gay and one is married. Their researchers are ter-
rible. It's a good thing they don't know I'm here; a successful businessman under thirty and the grandson of
a *conte*, you'd be at the top of the list.'

She'd wiped the shock off her face; all she showed
was mild amusement. If Luca hadn't heard the muffled
cry of anguish, he wouldn't have thought she was affected at all.

'Is it true?'

She shrugged. 'Does it matter?' She shook her head.
'Probably. Clara was always around, although Joe swore
they were just friends. Obviously. They were at Cam-
bridge together, and her father was party royalty; together they'll be unbeatable.'

She reached over and grabbed the iPad from him. 'I
told you, I'm a starter fiancée; they all meet their perfect match after we split up.' She scrolled down the article then tilted the screen towards him to show photos

of two very different men, each with a female companion. The younger of the two men was posed with his arm stiffly round a woman in her early twenties. She had a haughty, well-bred air, her long, straight hair held back from her high forehead with a thick Alice band.

'She really dresses like that,' Minty said. 'I think she was born in tweed and wellies.' She looked wistfully at the photo. 'They look good together, don't they?'

Luca murmured noncommittally. So this was Barty, the boy she had become engaged to so soon after fleeing from his bed? He looked…nice, affable: floppy hair, nice smile, laid-back. Unthreatening. He was just a boy.

But she had been just a girl.

'I never really fit in,' Minty continued. 'I tried, but I just don't have the whole pony club, hunt balls thing going for me. Taffy is a natural. They have three children already; can you imagine?' She slanted a glance at him. 'Shame you didn't meet her first.'

'She looks a little stern for me,' Luca said, studying the picture.

'Oh, yes, she rules poor Barty with a rod of iron. Not that he seems to mind.'

Luca moved the screen to enlarge the photo of the second man. A good twenty years older than Luca, he had a mass of long, greying hair, his skinny body squeezed into tight, black leather trousers. He was gazing adoringly at the much younger, taller, glossy, high-cheekboned woman on his arm with a look that suggested all his Christmases had come at once. 'This must be Spike?'

Minty nodded. 'Yes, bachelor number two. Actually, I think Spike has split up with his supermodel wife already. He's turning into a parody of an aging rock star.

But Barty's still happily married. I must send Joe a card, and maybe flowers. Remind me, will you?'

She was magnificent. All signs of pain had been wiped away; anyone walking in would think she really only felt mild interest in her ex-fiancé's very public new relationship. But Luca knew differently. And that knowledge changed everything. It was time to armour up, to grab his sword and shield. Luca Di Tore was going to play the knight yet again.

Maybe this time it would all be different

'Let's do something wild and crazy—go in a couple of hours late. Do you want to take a walk?'

Minty stared at Luca in astonishment. 'Go in late?' she repeated. 'Won't there be a national panic if you're not there on the dot of nine? They'll send the air force and the army here to make sure you're okay. Special Branch will abseil through the windows; there will be camera crews stampeding the house. But sure, I'd love to.'

Luca didn't respond to her nonsense. Instead he was staring at her shoes with undisguised disapproval. 'Do you need to change those?' Minty swallowed back a smile. She'd only brought ballet flats and flip-flops with her. Luca seemed fixated on the unsuitability of her footwear; it was as if she was wobbling along on six-inch bondage heels.

She was tempted to buy some, just to see his face.

'As long as you don't expect me to wade through fords or climb mountains, I think these will survive.' Minty strode over to the door, then turned back to say with perfect, limpid innocence, 'I am beginning to think you have some kind of anti-shoe fetish. You disapprove of every pair I own.'

'I took Francesca to Roma once,' Luca said. 'She

brought two large bags for a three-night stay and only the most ridiculously high heels. She then complained bitterly the whole time about her feet, about blisters, and when I offered to buy her some walking shoes she cried.'

Minty bit back a smile. 'I'm beginning to sympathise with poor Francesca. Was that the last straw?'

'Scuzi?'

'Your break-up. Was it over shoes or over your lack of sympathy?'

His mouth quirked. 'Maybe it was both. It should have been a romantic weekend. We had a five-star hotel right by the Spanish steps, the weather was perfect, but we fought the whole time. I had a much better time when I took you.'

His expression was unreadable and Minty swallowed, unsure what the floating feeling in her stomach meant. 'That was one of the best days of my life,' she said.

It had been. Sometimes she thought that that was the day her crush on Luca had turned from something inconvenient but entertaining into something real, all-encompassing. Or maybe the day he took pity on a small, sobbing girl and entertained her patiently, playing board games in a language he'd barely spoken. Minty had cheated dreadfully, of course, but he didn't seem to mind. Most days she could write him off as serious, stuffy, dull. And then he would do something kind, something spontaneous.

Would get under her skin.

Luca was still looking at her intently and all Minty wanted to do was to take a step towards him. Forget Joe, forget everything. For a moment she stood wavering, memories flooding through her. Memories of

Rome, of laughter and teasing, of being treated like an adult, treated with respect. Other memories pushed insistently: memories of firelight and red wine, tears kissed away, comforting arms becoming stronger, more dangerous. Heat.

And then the utter chill of rejection.

Minty turned resolutely away. 'Come on, then,' she called over her shoulder. 'Or you might not make it in till lunch, and even Special Ops wouldn't cope with that!'

He might be just a little bit biased but Luca knew that his farm was the most beautiful place on earth. The meadows were already strewn with a rainbow assortment of spring flowers; herds of cows were dotted about the distant fields, all chewing contentedly.

Minty sighed, a great, satisfied gust. 'When I'm in London I think it's the nicest place on earth and can't imagine living anywhere else,' she said. 'And when I'm at the ancestral pile I feel exactly the same way—I *yearn* for London. But this kind of countryside is different. It's peaceful and yet alive somehow. You know?'

Luca grunted in acknowledgement and kept on walking, faster than before. Minty had to break into a stride in order to keep up. He gave the velvet flip-flops a meaningful glance but manfully resisted saying anything.

He didn't know *what* to say. Things suddenly seemed different, almost comfortable. The moment he had said she could stay had felt like the start of something new between them. Or was it the moment she had let her facade crack a little, had let him in enough to see the hurt? Was that why he felt catapulted into deeper intimacy with her?

He had promised himself it wouldn't happen. Not again. And yet in some ways it was as inevitable as the dew-soaked dawn.

Besides, she was older now, and different under that flippant exterior. Maybe the depths he had always hoped for did exist after all.

Or maybe he was a fool who never learned.

He shook his head to clear his thoughts, searching for a neutral topic of conversation. 'I am going to a charity event in Florence this weekend—at least, my grandfather has summoned me there.' His mouth twisted wryly. 'You know the *conte*; he doesn't like the word *no*.'

'I love Florence,' Misty said wistfully. 'I haven't been there for years.'

He grimaced. 'I hate it: tourists, crammed streets, noise, expectations.' The hideous formality, the eternal disappointment of his grandfather. The only times Florence had been bearable were when Minty had tagged along. Her irreverence had always taken the sting out of his grandfather's disapproval.

She had almost made it fun.

'You're still not close to your grandfather?'

That was an understatement.

'He was always nice to me,' she continued, looking up at him, concern in her eyes—concern for him. That was unexpected.

And surprisingly nice.

'He approved of you: title, lots of well-connected relatives, the right manners—when you chose to show them. Me, however; I was a disappointment. No social aspirations. All I wanted to do was grub about on the farm or work in the factory.'

'Glad that someone approves of me. Maybe I should ask him to adopt me.'

'He'd accept like a shot,' Luca said. He stopped and turned, looked down at her, a sudden wild idea springing fully formed into his head. Minty was right, his grandfather had always liked her. 'Come with me.'

A faint colour crept over her cheeks. 'To please your grandfather?'

Was it? 'Maybe. Partly.' His eyes met hers, gold on blue.

Or was it because he liked having her around, liked the way she made him feel? Because with her he felt something other than responsibility, something a lot lighter.

Because when he looked into those improbably blue eyes he felt like he could do anything, be anyone. Since his parents' crash he had worked so hard to be responsible, sensible, to live up to their legacy. His eyes had been so fixed on his chosen path he'd never noticed the small, winding diversions tempting him away.

Except just occasionally, in the company of the willowy girl standing next to him. Then he occasionally allowed himself to explore other routes, just for a little while, until his feet found his chosen straight-and-narrow path again.

He missed those diversions.

For a moment the world fell away. She could have been anywhere: desert, city street, her father's estate. All that existed was the heat of those extraordinary eyes, suddenly alight again with fire, passion. With life.

Minty swallowed, trying to get some moisture back into a suddenly dry mouth. His gaze scorched her and she felt the heat of it right down to her toes, pooling at the pit of her stomach, molten lava burning her up inside.

She took a tentative step towards him, despite the

warning bell clanging in her head. This man was different. She had survived the others; she might not survive this one. Not again. But now she had made the move she didn't know if she could, if she wanted to, pull back.

Only she didn't have to. He did, stepping back, moving away, pulling his eyes abruptly away from hers, breaking the connection. The shutters were back down and he was once again her childhood adversary, the disapproving golden boy.

It was a good thing he'd stopped, otherwise she most definitely would have, she told herself, but the ache of frustrated desire was hot and insistent.

He started walking again, further down into the valley. Minty stood for a second, watching him: the tall, broad frame; the dark hair, dishevelled as if he had washed it this morning and just left it to dry. He probably had.

Awareness prickled up and down her spine. Dear God, she wanted to find out if he really was all that she remembered. She wanted to pull that T-shirt up over his shoulders; undo his belt with trembling, suddenly clumsy fingers; try to unbutton his jeans before impatiently yanking them down. She wanted to see him, taste him, feel his skin against hers. She leant helplessly against the fence, her legs suddenly incapable of movement.

This impulsive nature of hers. She needed to contain it, channel it elsewhere into work and projects. No more throwing herself at unsuitable men, trying to be what they wanted. No more failing.

She was attracted to Luca. Okay, people were attracted to other people all the time. That didn't mean you had to act on it, throw yourself all in. That kind of behaviour led to multiple marriages, multiple engagements, broken hearts and ruined expectations. She could be better than that. She didn't have to take up the mantle of her inheritance.

And yet…it could be so easy. She knew what he wanted; he'd made it so clear. And she could be that hard-working, country-loving, family-orientated girl. For a short while. After all, she'd already played the hunt ball, point-to-point country girl; the wild and crazy rock chick; the hard-working and politically passionate small business owner.

The ironic thing was that she was all of the above, a bit of her, at least. Just as she was also a shopaholic, a traveller, a reader, a lover of trash TV, a baker, a party girl, a veg-out queen; just as she loved takeaway food and posh restaurants. She was lots of things. But nobody was interested in the contrasts and the contradictions; they wanted her pigeonholed and pinned down.

Luca stopped and looked back. 'Are you coming?' he called.

What would he do if she sauntered down the hill, walked right up to him and put that swing in her hips she could do so well? If she pressed herself close, raised herself up on her tiptoes, pressed her mouth against his? Would he push her away, lose himself in her for a few moments, hours, then regret it? Would he allow her to morph into his perfect woman until he finally saw through her or she couldn't pretend any more?

She wasn't prepared to find out.

'Just admiring the view,' she called back, allowing a flirtatious edge to creep into her voice, a smile to curve on her lips. Just because she had decided not to go and get him didn't mean she didn't want him to admire her. She was only human, after all.

She took her time walking along the path towards

him. The stone path had turned first to gravel and now to grass, lightly lined with woodchips to protect against the mud. It took them in a straight line through the fields, larger, more rolling fields than the patchwork style she was used to at home, all seamlessly making up the same landscape, broken only by small trees or hedgerows.

And Luca, an integral part of this pastoral landscape, linked by blood, work and love. Minty was just an on-looker, a walk-on part in somebody else's life. Again.

CHAPTER SIX

'IT'S NOT THAT I'm not enjoying the walk,' Minty said when she reached him, 'but I am wondering where we're heading.'

Luca glanced at her curiously. 'I thought you were a spur-of-the-moment type girl?'

She flushed. 'Usually, yes. I mean, I have been known to do the odd impulsive thing. But there's usually a reason or a destination. If I suddenly decide I'm going to crew a tall yacht around the world, for instance, then there is a plan behind that impulsive decision. I don't just get on a boat to see where it sails.'

There was still a questioning look on his face. 'Did you really crew a tall yacht round the world?'

'Yes,' she said. 'At least, halfway round the world. I signed off when I got to Australia. A last minute decision that some *might* have called impulsive, but I knew exactly where I was heading and why.'

Luca raised an eyebrow. Minty knew full well he'd spent the summer he'd turned fourteen perfecting the art. It didn't make the effect any less devastating. 'Where were you heading?'

'To Sydney,' she admitted. 'To party and to learn to surf. Turns out boat crewing was really hard work.'

His mouth twitched and Minty reined in the undignified urge to stick her tongue out at him. 'So,' she prompted. 'Where are we going?'

'The cow sheds are in that direction.' He gestured down the valley. 'Or we could head over the fields towards the stream.' His eyes flickered towards her feet.

Minty followed his eyes and sighed. The bright velvet was looking dusty and stained, beyond repair, not that she would admit it. 'Not one more word about my shoes,' she said. 'They'll cope.' She glanced over the fields to the trees lining the horizon. 'I haven't been down to the stream for years. It was always one of my favourite spots—and, let's face it, way more picturesque than a cow shed, even a cow shed that produces wonderful milk to make into even more wonderful *gelato*. I vote we head that way.'

He nodded and strode off without waiting to see if she was following. It was, Minty thought, a good thing that she was long-legged, otherwise she'd have had to scuttle to keep up with him. And that would have been most undignified.

She caught up with the tall Italian and fell into step beside him, arms swinging, unabashedly enjoying the air, the sun, the exercise. She looked around her with approval. The views had been glorious from the farmhouse, but as they approached the bottom of the valley the countryside was not just a view, something to admire—it enclosed them; they were a part of it.

It wasn't silent; it was too real for that. A cacophony of birds competed with each other to make the loudest call, sing the most tuneful song, like some avian reality show. She almost expected to see a row of small feathered judges sitting on a branch ready to destroy the enthusiastic chirpers' dreams. She could hear the sound of engines in the distance—some farm machinery doing something she probably wouldn't be able to identify if she stood and watched for an hour—mingled with the ever-present lowing of the cattle.

Definitely not quiet, but somehow so peaceful. In just a few weeks the corn poppies would explode into a vibrant slash of red in the green landscape. She wanted to be around to see it.

'I am usually all about the city,' she said. 'Yet this place is so special too. I missed it. No wonder you wanted to stay here. You must love it that it's yours, part of you.'

Luca nodded. 'It's part of the family history, in my blood. It's a good marketing gimmick too; all the milk we produce is used in our ice cream, although we have to buy in a lot more. It's tenanted out, though, I don't get involved in the day-to-day work much.'

Judging by the firm muscles under the snug jeans and T-shirt Minty suspected he did more than he let on. If sitting at a desk and testing ice cream led to bodies like that, London's gyms would be a lot less full. And a lot less sweaty.

The sun was still shining down from the cloudless sky bathing the earth below in a benevolent warmth, yet Minty's arm goose-pimpled and she suppressed a sudden shiver. Walking with this man, in this place, suddenly filled her with a melancholy, a lonely nostalgia.

A babble of shallow water interrupted her thoughts, and pushing through a line of small trees brought Minty to the edge of a wide, shallow stream liberally carpeted with pebbles and rocks. Luca was leaning against a tall oak tree, staring thoughtfully into the water.

'There won't be any fish in there,' Minty said, walking next to him and following his eyeline. 'Too shallow.'

'I didn't know you fished.'

'I don't.' She shuddered. 'Too much sitting around

for me. And I always feel so sorry for them, with their mouths gaping and their cold little eyes. Daddy fished, of course. I think he almost has to; it's in the earl charter or something.'

She stopped, looking down at the shallow water. 'Spike liked country sports too. In some ways he and Daddy were better suited than he and I. You know, I watch some of those TV programmes about music. Spike was so anti-establishment when he was young, all about the shock value and creativity. And now he has a country estate, fishes and wears tweed. I kid you not. And loads of his friends are the same. The ones who didn't die of drug overdoses, that is. They don't even see the irony.'

'Are you still friends?'

She shook her head. 'Not at all; he didn't want to be friends.' She sighed, almost imperceptibly. 'They never do.'

For a moment he didn't say anything, just stood there, a reassuring presence. The silence was oddly comforting.

'Come on, Minty, accompany me to Florence.'

Her heart gave a funny little jump. It felt almost like hope. What harm could there be in a weekend away?

'A couple of days in Florence would be nice. And...' she gave him her best cheeky smile '...grandfathers usually love me. Grandmothers not so much, but we can't have everything.' She eyed him suspiciously, trying to remain objective, not to allow her gaze to dwell on the stubbled cheeks and the way his hair fell unguarded over his forehead.

'Why do you want me to?'

'Does there have to be a reason?'

For Luca? Usually yes, unless he felt sorry for her, just like the old days.

She didn't want to be the object of his pity.

He shrugged. 'He does like you. I know I shouldn't care about pleasing him and, to be honest, I find it insulting that he will be far more impressed if you accompany me to this event than he is by my multi-million-euro turnover, but…' He paused, oddly vulnerable. 'But he's old. Frail.' Another pause, longer this time, then, almost imperceptibly, 'He and Gio are all I have left.'

Minty was torn between conflicting emotions. If there was one subject she didn't do, it was families. Oh, she could laugh at her own situation, turn her childhood, her failed relationships, into a self-deprecating stand-up routine that had them rolling in the aisle. But deep, heartfelt, emotional discussions? Not her style. And yet, she sensed that this man rarely opened up, that he carried his shame, his fears, tightly boxed up inside him.

For some unfathomable reason he was choosing here and now to release them—he was choosing her. It terrified her and yet at the same time she was touched, gratified that he didn't think she was too shallow to understand.

'He's a link to your mother,' she offered shyly.

'Yes!' He turned to her. 'Exactly. Would she approve of me, of the man I've become? Or, like him, would she be disappointed that I don't attend balls and charity events and the opera in Verona? Would she think I was an uncouth country farmer who thinks of nothing but ice cream?'

'She married a farmer,' Minty pointed out. 'And for what it's worth I think she would be ridiculously proud of you. So proud she'd have to bite her tongue at parties so as not to bore all the other guests with a long list of your virtues! I think she would look at you and see a man proud of his home and his heritage. A man who has no reason at all to make his grandfather happy, but wants to anyway, because that's the kind of person he is. That's what she would see.'

Minty stopped abruptly, heat flushing her cheeks. Where on earth had all that come from? 'Anyway,' she said gruffly. 'That's what I think. For what it's worth.'

Consumed with embarrassment, she couldn't look at him. Instead, kicking off her shoes, she padded forward, enjoying the unaccustomed feel of the soft spring grass under her bare feet, still pale from months of London winter, from the restriction of tights, thick socks and boots. The stream rushed merrily on over the flat pebbles, a cool, enticing blue. Minty dipped one toe in and inhaled in shock. Goodness, it was cold.

'It's not just about you, though. These occasions—charity balls, trips to the opera—they're all good for networking.' She shrugged, leaning forward until all her weight was on the submerged foot, wiggling it over the flat pebbles until it was comfortable. She dipped her other foot in until she was standing in the stream, water swirling round her ankles. 'It all depends,' she said, horribly aware that he still hadn't spoken. 'Depends on what you want to do. I'm happy to go with you. It could be a good business step. You should start to think about sponsorship opportunities as well. It's the missing link in your marketing strategy.'

She swivelled to face him and instantly wished she hadn't. If he looked this good in a black T-shirt, what on earth would he be like in black tie? Her pulse sped up.

Minty shuffled backwards, carefully testing her weight on the pebble bed before shifting. Her skin had adjusted to the temperature; it was gloriously refreshing. Bending down, she trailed her fingers in the water. 'I wish it was deep enough to swim in.'

He was giving her a quizzical look. 'It must be freezing. Is this one of those English things?'

'Used to be. Of course, now we're not supposed to swim in rivers; if it's not private land or contaminated, then the health and safety people will get you. Luckily there's a river at Westhorpe which has a perfect bathing place. With the great British weather, though, there's no point waiting for a nice day. If we did, we'd never swim.' She heaved a gusty sigh. 'Of course, I didn't spend enough holidays there to really take advantage of it and I doubt Stepmama lets the heir, spare and girl loose in it often.'

'I prefer a nice, clean, regulated swimming pool myself,' Luca said a little stiffly, but she noticed that his eyes seemed to be drawn to the calves of her legs, her submerged ankles.

Regulated pool indeed. 'Come in,' she coaxed. 'The water's lovely.'

He shook his head at her, amused. 'You said yourself it's not deep enough to swim in; it barely covers your feet!'

'I'm paddling,' she said with as much dignity as was possible when one is standing in the middle of a stream. 'And it's lovely.' She swivelled round to show him, almost slipping on an unwary pebble but catching herself in time. 'See?' Her eyes were laughing at him, daring him, but she felt secure. He seemed so solid on the bank, so rooted in the ground she couldn't imagine him doing something so uncivilised, so childlike. 'Scared?' she taunted softly.

Slowly, with almost cat-like grace, Luca pushed himself away from the tree on which he'd been leaning and leant down, loosening the ties on his boot before slipping it off, casually kicking it off his foot. His eyes fixed on Minty's face, he slid his sock off his foot, tucking it neatly into a boot. It should have looked ridiculous, *he* should have looked ridiculous, like a still from a fifties seaside advertisement: father relaxing at the beach. But there was something so deliberate, so assured in his movements, Minty could only stand and watch, her mouth dry.

Now the other shoe, the other sock. His eyes still on hers, he pulled up his T-shirt, flashing a glimpse of toned stomach. He loosened his belt and then slowly, far, far too slowly, worked the buttons at his fly before pulling off the jeans and laying them neatly on the ground.

Minty stared at his legs, her mouth dry. They were, she thought, rather nice legs; very nice indeed. Defined; definitely legs that had known manual work, legs with lean, muscular strength, but not bulky. They had a shapeliness that any regency buck would have been glad to slip into a pair of skintight breeches. They were less tanned than his hands and his face, more a burnt-gold colour, lightly dusted with silky dark hairs.

Her eyes skated back up over the crisp, blue boxers, up that narrow waist and the disappointingly hidden abdomen she'd caught such a tantalisingly small glimpse of earlier. Up to the comforting width of his shoulders and his strong, golden arms.

Minty swallowed. As Luca advanced over the grass, his eyes fixed on her face, she wanted to retreat, wade backwards through the icy water, flee to the safety of the other bank. But she was paralysed. The sun was behind him, casting a glow to that golden flesh. His amber eyes were lit up with amusement, with challenge. With desire. She wanted to speak, to break the spell, but she was caught; there was nothing she could do.

Tension mingled with the sweet ache of desire twisting in her chest, spreading outwards, downwards. She swayed helplessly as he slid one foot into the water. His expression didn't change, didn't register the cold. Her heart raced, the beat so loud, thrumming in her ears. It was as if the countryside marched to the beat of her desire. Slowly, so very slowly he advanced, wading effortlessly through the shallow depths.

Minty licked her lips, desperately trying to get some moisture back into her dry mouth. A flicker of his eyes showed his register of the movement—and his approval. Her hands, shaking, damp, twisted convulsively.

Luca stood before her, impossibly tall, imposing. Infinitely fascinating. She wanted to lean bonelessly into him, be absorbed by him—by his strength, by his goodness, by his loyalty. She couldn't help herself. She raised one hand to his sculpted cheek and traced a feather-light path down, past the indention of the dimple, onto his lips. How could anything be simultaneously so hard and yet so soft? She ran her finger wonderingly along his smooth lower lip, coming to rest on his jaw.

There it was, faint but determined, the muscle tensing: a give-away that he was not as calm as he seemed. She took one tiny step closer, the water swirling round her ankles, the sharp cold a welcome relief on her sensitised skin. That one tiny step brought her into full contact with him. Her breasts, swollen, aching, pressed against his chest. Leg against leg, arm against arm. Minty looked up at him and saw such unfettered desire swelling in the tawny depths of his eyes that she was undone.

'Luca,' she said hoarsely.

He didn't answer but looked down at her searchingly. What the question was she did not know, but her face must have signalled an answer because with a muttered groan Luca pulled her close, moulding her long curves against his hard body, one hand tilting her chin up as his mouth came down upon hers.

The urgency of his embrace took her by surprise. This was no teasing kiss but a wholesale assault on her weakened defences. His mouth was hard and sure on hers, his hands holding her close, caressing. He was in control, completely in control, and she was being swept away. She pressed harder against him, one hand clutching at his shoulder, the other slipping behind his head to bury into the thick, dark hair.

Time came to a standstill. All she knew was this: his mouth on hers; the sure, steady hands tracing such long, languorous circles on her back setting her skin on fire beneath the fine material of her dress. The thin layer of cotton felt as thick as a blanket separating her thirsty skin from his touch. Unsteadily she pushed him away, pulling her dress over her head, ready to fling it down. She looked wildly around for somewhere safe, somewhere dry, to put it, her fingers itching to start pulling at Luca's shirt. There must be somewhere...

Then it hit her. They were standing in the middle of a stream and, despite her earlier protestations, a cold stream. She looked ruefully up at Luca. 'Nowhere to put this.'

He looked back at her, the heat still blazing in his eyes. 'Not a problem,' he said and, before Minty could move, he swooped her up and carried her to the bank, stepping out of the stream and laying her underneath a wide-spread tree. Luca stood looking at her for one long, torturous moment. She met his gaze fearlessly, openly letting her need and want shine out. And then he covered her body with his. Her mouth was his and she was swept away in a tangled heat of kisses and caresses. There was nothing but him and the heat blazing between them. There was no sound but their gasps and moans. Nothing but the here and the now. Nothing but them.

CHAPTER SEVEN

Luca Di Tore strode up the narrow alleyway, scrutinising the numbers on the walls on either side. It was typical of Minty, he thought, to do Florence in her own idiosyncratic way, turning down both the Conte's offer of hospitality and Luca's own suggestion that they enjoy the privacy of a hotel.

Staying separately wasn't all bad, though. There were bound to be rumours if they were spotted together and he wasn't ready for that. *They* weren't ready for that. It was too new, too fragile, too unknown. And that was scary. Luca didn't really do unknown.

For eighteen years he had been solid, dependable, safe. Standing ankle-deep in a stream wasn't skydiving but it was a start. It was unplanned, spontaneous.

Being with *her* was unplanned, was spontaneous.

There were so many reasons that it was wrong. So many reasons not to continue. But standing by that stream he had been utterly helpless. He might have turned her down once before, resisted her once before, but he only had so much willpower. He had used it all up where Minty Davenport was concerned.

So this was a diversion and that was fine. This time he was not going to plan ahead, look for troubles that might never even arise. This time he was going to go along for the ride and see where the road took him.

It wasn't as if there was any future together; they both knew that. She would get bored soon enough, be on to the next thing; long term he wanted, he needed, stability.

As he reached the end of the alleyway it opened out, not into the street but into a small square of three-storey painted buildings. It should have felt overcast, claustrophobic, but, set about with vibrant pots of coloured flowers, hanging baskets on every wrought-iron balcony, it was welcoming and eclectic. Very Minty.

A narrow stone staircase curved up the side of the nearest building, the number on the side corresponding to that of the paper in his hand. Luca straightened his bow tie. All he knew about Magdalena was that Minty had stayed with her the summer she'd spent in Florence.

The summer before Rose had died.

He sensed Minty didn't give her affection that easily but she obviously adored this woman. Luca wanted to make a good impression.

'Luca!' Looking up, his heart jolted. It was less than twenty-four hours since they had arrived in Florence, less than twenty-four hours since he had dropped her off in a square north of the Arno, at her insistence. She'd had a couple of things to get, she had insisted; she would walk over to the Oltrarno district where she was staying, just the other side of the River Arno.

'It'll be nice to have a wander after being cooped up in the car,' she'd said. 'Reacquaint myself with these old streets.' She'd looked around, beaming. 'Oh, it is nice to be back. How have I stayed away so long?'

Reluctant to leave her, Luca had offered to accompany her, but she'd insisted he go to his grandfather's villa in an exclusive suburb high on the hills behind the city. 'He's waiting for you,' she'd said. 'Don't keep him waiting, I'll be fine.'

And she evidently was. Hanging over the iron railing, her face lit up with excitement, she looked no older than a schoolgirl. 'Come and see what Magdalena's done,' she called. 'She's made you a snack. I hope you're hungry; Magdalena is incapable of producing anything less than a banquet, but I thought this thing tonight would probably be all canapés and no substance and you'd be glad of a meal.'

Her excited chatter guided him up to the narrow terrace overlooking the square only to come to an abrupt halt as he finally faced her. Her eyes widened, an appreciative glow in them as she looked him up and down in a way that made him want to drag the pretty floral sundress off her right there on the balcony.

'Wow' was all she said, still looking slightly stunned. 'You scrub up nicely.' She whistled.

Luca adjusted the cuffs of his dress suit. 'You've seen me in suits before,' he teased.

'I know you like to live in suits. Personally, I thought nothing could top the jeans and black T-shirt, or at least you out of the jeans and black T-shirt, but this...' Her eyes swept up and down, lingering on his legs, his shoulders, his chest. 'I like it.'

'I don't look like a waiter?'

'Not at all. Well, a very sexy, desirable waiter. Come on.' And, grabbing his hand, she pulled him into the high-ceilinged, cool apartment.

Luca barely had time to take in the large, tastefully furnished living room with French doors flung open to the balcony beyond before being pulled through the door and along a wooden-floored passage and into a small gallery-style kitchen. The kitchen also had French doors opening onto the other side of the building and Minty, her hand still in his, led the way towards them, opening them properly so they could exit side by side onto the private terrace beyond.

Two chairs were pulled up round a small wrought-iron table, its top barely visible below a platter heaped with food. A cold beer was already poured into a frosted glass, the chair pulled slightly out.

'Go on, sit,' she said.

Luca sat, touched at the care she had taken, his appreciation tinged with amusement at her palpable excitement. 'Is this for me?' he asked, indicating the beer. She nodded.

'You're not driving tonight, are you? I know there will be wine at the gala but I thought you might appreciate something a bit more refreshing first.'

'I do, thank you.'

He took an appreciative gulp of the cool, slightly fizzy liquid and looked over at the platter. Minty was right; a man could not exist on canapés alone. And, after she and the absent Magdalena had gone to so much trouble, well, it would be rude not to sample their work.

As they ate, they talked. Minty chattered on about her previous evening catching up with her old landlady and the day she had spent shopping. 'I have the most divine dress for tonight,' she told him. 'Wait till you see it.' In the small gaps between her chatter, Luca filled her in on the uncomfortably formal evening he had spent with his grandfather and several aunts, uncles and cousins and his day spent mostly working as far away from his irascible grandfather as possible.

'Luckily there was plenty to do,' he said, grinning

across at his attentive companion. 'I seem to have rather neglected things the past couple of days.'

'All work and no play,' she murmured with a provocative smile. 'Speaking of which, have you finished?' Minty was on her feet, the lines of her body visible through the thin fabric of her dress.

Luca nodded. 'Delicious.'

She padded towards him on bare feet, leant over him and wound her arms around his neck. He could feel her breath on his cheek, the lemon scent of her shampoo and something warmer, earthier, distinctly Minty. A jolt of desire shot through him. 'I hope you have a little appetite for pudding,' she whispered. 'Magdalena is out for the afternoon.'

He pulled her down onto his knee, enjoying the silk of her skin under his touch, the fineness of her bones. 'It depends on the type of pudding,' he said softly against her shoulder, feeling her shudder as his hand moved over the bare skin.

'Only the wickedest type, of course,' she breathed. 'But not here. Come on; I want to show you my new dress.'

Luca allowed her to hop out of his lap and pull him up. He spun her round to face him. 'A new dress doesn't sound that appetising,' he said, capturing her mouth with his. She sunk into the embrace for a dizzying second then stepped back.

'Ah, but I went lingerie shopping as well...' And, throwing a saucy smile over her shoulder, she sauntered back into the house. Luca watched her move, the swish of the long skirt around her legs, the movement of her hair bouncing with her stride, the provocative swish of her hips. He smiled appreciatively and followed her into the apartment.

New lingerie sounded enticing; stripping her of it even more so. He quickened his stride. There were still a couple of hours before the benefit started; he wanted to make sure they made full use of every single second.

It was a little ironic, Minty thought, that she was doing her best to shake off her socialite image, yet here she was, at the sort of benefit duty occasionally compelled her to attend back home. Swap the conversation into English and the Prosecco to champagne, and she could be back in London.

This should have been the last place she wanted to be, yet to be here with Luca felt right. Disturbingly so. She looked over to where he stood making polite conversation with one of his grandfather's friends.

He looked completely relaxed, his glass held in one hand, polite interest on his face. Oh, he might claim to hate this part of his life—society galas, charity events, the great and the good all gathered together in a self-congratulatory way—but he suited it. Just as he suited the quiet life in the country, as he suited running his company quietly but decisively confident.

Maybe he was a chameleon, like her. But, no; Minty had stopped believing in a perfect match a long time ago. You changed yourself to suit the one you loved and hoped it was enough, or you kept going, spinning through a carousel of different partners to suit each stage in your life. Romantic? No. Practical? Yes.

She had vowed she was done with romance, had promised herself not to get pulled under again. But Luca, her gallant knight with the startling eyes, had the potential to pull her deeper than she had ever gone before. Minty suppressed a shiver despite the almost oppressive heat in the crowded old room.

As if he could read her thoughts, Luca caught her eye and raised his glass to her in a silent salute. Minty took a sip of her Prosecco and smiled back before turning back to her elegant companion, the wife of one of Luca's cousins, to continue making polite conversation.

But, although she could smile, nod and make polite replies, her mind was far away. Back in Oschia by the stream; reliving the afternoon's tryst at her apartment. She knew she and Luca had chemistry. It had been fiery when she was eighteen and clueless; now it was combustible.

She had to be careful that she didn't get too caught up in the flames. She wasn't very good at separating her heart and body—and she had never experienced this level of heat before.

Maybe, just maybe, he had been right to call a halt all those years ago. She couldn't have handled him then, although it hurt to admit it. She had been far too naive, for all her veneer of sophistication.

To be honest, she wasn't too sure she could handle it now. Not the sex—that she could definitely manage. It was more the way he looked at her, the way he made her feel: safe.

She was used to being desired, wanted. This was infinitely more dangerous.

Minty took a deep breath, trying to quell the sudden rush of panic. She shouldn't worry about Luca; she was on her guard. They had a finite time and she had put a lock on her heart. This relationship—no, this fling—was all about the fun. She'd walked away from him before; she could do it again.

'Ready to go?' Minty jumped as Luca came up behind her, at the gentle brush of his hands on her bare shoulders. A shiver ran through her at his touch.

'I'm the guest; I'm at your command,' she replied, drawing the words out long and low, and had the pleasure of seeing his eyes dilate at her words.

'Then I'm definitely ready to go,' he said, his hands tightening momentarily on her shoulders. 'I've talked business, you charmed my grandfather; I think we have fulfilled our duties admirably.'

Minty tossed her hair. 'I told you grandfathers were my speciality.'

Luca bent over and kissed her neck. 'I was rather hoping grandsons were,' he said softly against her ear.

'Depends on the grandson,' she replied, and walked off towards the ballroom exit. She didn't look back. Right here, right now she was sure of him, she knew he would be following her. She left the glittering room full of the cream of Florentine society and descended the old stone staircase to the grand foyer below, where they had left their coats.

'If I hold your hand will I be acting like the perfect escort or overstepping our agreement to keep our private lives hidden?' Luca asked as he helped Minty into her coat. She laughed; put like that, it did sound ridiculous.

'We're in Florence, so act away,' she said and held her hand out to him and he took it. His hand was large, comforting. It would have felt safe if the skin-on-skin contact didn't make her tingle everywhere.

'Where to, my lady?'

'Can we walk just for a bit?' Minty asked. 'One of my favourite Italian traditions is watching people promenade. It's too cold in London and, on the rare occasion it's not, watching people stagger drunkenly down the street isn't quite the same thing. Look.' She held up one of her wedge-heeled shoes. 'I even have sensible footwear on.'

'Seven inches of heel is not sensible, no matter how the heel is styled,' Luca grumbled.

Minty shot him a limpid glance. 'Typical male exaggeration. These heels are three inches at the most, but we'll call it seven if it pleases you.' She squealed as Luca swung her round, pulling her hard against him.

'You seemed satisfied earlier.'

His mouth hovered temptingly above hers. Minty stood on her tiptoes, trying to reach it, but he moved it fractionally away, tantalisingly out of her reach. 'I'm sorry,' she said, trying to look contrite. 'You are of course magnificent in every way. A love machine of the highest order.'

Luca quirked an eyebrow at her. 'Seven inches doesn't even begin to do justice,' she continued, trying to look serious, her smirk threatening to break out any second. She made her eyes big, pleading. 'Please say you forgive me?'

His mouth descended onto hers and for the next few moments all Minty was aware of was him. The bunch of his muscles under her roaming hands, the hardness of his mouth, the way he felt, smelt, overloaded all her senses. The sound of teasing voices brought her out of her sensual stupor. She pulled back.

'Not in the street! You, at least, were brought up much better than that.'

'We could go back to yours?' he suggested, his eyes molten gold with desire.

Minty shook her head. 'Magdalena will be back. Besides, you promised me a promenade, and a promenade is what I want.'

'Then a promenade you shall have,' Luca promised.

* * *

'You don't know this city at all,' she accused Luca with a grin when he took them the wrong way for the third time.

'Maybe I just want to get you alone in a dark alley-way,' he suggested.

'Good try. Come on, I told you it was this way.'

'I never come here as a tourist,' he explained. 'I stay at the *conte*'s villa, which is outside the city. We are driven to parties and restaurants. Obviously I have been inside every museum, every church, every park, but I've never had the freedom to walk around like this.'

'Not even with Francesca?' Minty asked, wishing she'd not spoken the moment she'd done so. She sounded dangerously like a jealous girlfriend, which she wasn't—jealous, or indeed a girlfriend.

He laughed. 'Francesca? Wander round the streets without a purpose or someone to impress? No, she would have made me stay at that gala until the last moment, and then escort the *conte* home so she could be seen leaving with him.'

'I like him,' Minty said, wanting to change the subject. 'Your grandfather, I mean. And I think...' She cast about for the right words but ended up saying baldy, 'I think he is really proud of you.'

'You got all that from a five-minute conversation?' Luca sounded sceptical.

'I got that from five minutes of him singing your praises. Did you know that your *gelato* is the most authentic mass-produced product he has ever tasted?'

'It's traditionally made, not mass-produced—' Luca stopped mid-speech. 'The *conte* said that?'

Minty nodded. 'And much, much more, but I'd hate

for you to get big-headed. Aha! I told you this was the way.'

They were at the entrance to a large square, a fountain in the middle. Along one side was a two-storey building with a series of steps leading to the pillared terrace. At the back of the shallow terrace was a wall with heavy-looking doors interspersed at intervals. The pillars were impressively carved with round medallion-style decorations, a picture of a baby on each one.

'The hospital of the innocents,' Minty said softly. 'I used to come here most days, trying to imagine what it was like to know you had been literally posted into an orphanage. I wonder if it was better to grow up never knowing who your parents were or to know why you were here. Or—and spot the melodrama of a teenager here—was it worse to have parents who took no notice of you at all? These children had no expectations, no obligations; they were free…'

'Free to be foundlings, paupers and servants,' Luca said wryly. He put an arm around her. 'Is this what you did when you lived in Florence, mooched dreamily around here?'

Minty nestled into his embrace. 'I promenaded and flirted with dangerously attractive Italian boys.' She looked up at him provocatively. 'A habit I don't seem to have lost.' Luca's arm tightened round her shoulders. 'I went to every museum at least once and what felt like every church. I saw more depictions of the Madonna and Child than anybody could cope with and realised an art history degree wasn't for me, despite its royal connections!'

'What did you do instead?'

'Well, I did get engaged twice before I was twenty-one,' she pointed out. 'That took up some time.'

'And the boat to Australia,' he said.

'That came afterwards. I was running away from the fallout with Spike.' She sighed. 'I do seem to run away a lot.' She straightened up, moving out of his embrace. 'I shouldn't have brought you here; it always makes me sombre. Come on, I want *gelato*. Does anywhere round here stock yours?' She smiled at him. 'Ours, I should say.'

She grabbed his hand and pulled him along, away from the square and the gloomy thoughts it always evoked. 'All the really good *gelato* shops in Florence make their own,' Luca said. 'And they are all worth trying.' He flashed her a dangerously sexy grin. 'I'm not so vain that I can't appreciate somebody else's artisanship.'

Another couple of moments and they were outside one of the city's most popular *gelaterias*. The glass windows showcased the long counters filled with over one hundred vibrantly coloured ice creams.

'Cone or a cup?'

Minty gave Luca a withering glance. 'Oh, I know you purists are all about the cup, but I, my friend, am English and we eat our ice cream out of a cone. But,' she added cautiously, 'I am a sophisticated type and I only like sugar cones.'

'And which flavours would the beautiful *signorina* like in her sugar cone?'

'All of them,' she said, her nose pressed up against the glass like a starving Victorian waif. 'How can I choose?'

'Let's go in and decide,' Luca suggested. 'Or we could just stand here and look…'

It only took ten minutes for Minty to choose, which, as she explained to Luca, was pretty good, considering she had been in Italy for no more than a couple of weeks and had yet to enter a *gelateria*.

'You have been to my factory shop, like clockwork, every afternoon break,' Luca said indignantly.

'It's not the same,' Minty tried to explain.

'And yet with all this choice you go for a *frutti di bosco* and a lemon,' he said. Luca had spent some time trying to persuade Minty to be more exotic in her choice.

'It's a classic,' she said. 'I'm sure mint liquorice and coffee makes a great combination but I wanted something more subtle. And yes,' she added as she saw the glint in his eye, 'I can be subtle. Just look at me tonight.'

'You are beautiful tonight,' he said. 'I didn't forget to tell you that, did I?'

'You have only mentioned it ten or so times but I'll forgive you.' Normally Minty liked to live up to her public image and dress accordingly. She eschewed the fake tan and barely-there clothes of other party girls, preferring to stay at the cutting edge of fashion and to be a little less obvious.

Tonight, however, she had decided against *avant garde* design and had chosen something appropriate for a charity gala dinner, a soft dress of midnight-blue. The material was clingy and deceptively demure, high-necked and calf-length with chiffon shoulder straps. Not only did it cling to Minty's torso like a second skin, until the waist where it flared out into a ballerina skirt, but both the neckline and from the mid-thigh down were made of a thinner, almost transparent material, showcasing her legs and cleavage whilst covering them. She'd teamed it with a silver velvet wrap for outside and silver star earrings.

Simple yet devastating—at least, that was the effect

she had hoped for and, by the look in Luca's eyes when she had finally got dressed, she had achieved it.

They walked along side by side, not speaking as they enjoyed their ice cream, just content to be together. For once Minty didn't feel the need to interrupt the silence, to prattle or make jokes. She just *was*. They strolled down the side of the world-famous Uffizi towards the Arno and Minty caught Luca's arm, pulling him to a standstill. On the other side of the street a lone violinist was playing. They stood and listened to the soaring strings for a moment and then, by silent accord, sat on the steps opposite, enthralled by the magic of the night.

Her every sense was on fire, the bitter of the lemon contrasting with the sweetness of the berries; the feel of Luca nestled protectively by her side strong, comforting. The exquisite sound of the violin was high and almost unbearably poignant as it sang a yearning melody. Other people were walking by, and a few others had sat near them, but to Minty it felt as if the violinist was playing a serenade for Luca and her alone. She leant further into Luca, letting the whole weight of her body relax into him, shut her eyes and listened to the music. Whatever happened in the future, right here, right now, she was having a perfect moment.

And she wasn't alone.

'See, this is why I love Florence,' Minty said as the violinist made his final bow and, scooping in the coins and notes, prepared to pack up. 'You don't know what's round the corner.'

'A church?' suggested Luca solemnly. 'A museum?'

She nudged him. 'No! I was eighteen when I arrived here. I felt so free. You know I was dumped in school at seven, finishing school at sixteen. This is the first place where there were no expectations. Even the summers I came to you, there was a certain pressure to live up to my reputation.'

'And you haven't been back since?'

Minty shrugged. 'I don't know why I've stayed away, never shared it with anyone. I haven't had the chance to, I suppose. The Minty I am here didn't fit with the Minty I am elsewhere. The person people expect me to be.'

'What do you mean?' Luca's voice was soft, caressing, non-judgemental, and for once Minty resisted the temptation to turn her past into a comedy routine.

'Well, I got engaged, of course, pretty much straight away after going back to London.' She caught his eye and blushed. The memory of that time was inextricably bound up with the night she'd spent with him. 'I was grieving for Rose. I was so scared and alone. Then Barty proposed to me on his twenty-first birthday and, fool that I was, I said yes. I wasn't even nineteen. Honestly, a baby! Of course, he's a viscount, so it stirred up all kinds of silly society nonsense and publicity, even more so when I called it off.' She shivered as the memories engulfed her despite the warm breeze.

'Not only was I far too young, but that house…you can't imagine. It was like a museum and a mausoleum all rolled into one, with hundreds of aunts and grandparents all staring disapprovingly. Hideous. Barty wanted us to live there with the whole family. Very twinset and pearls and hunting; not at all me. About as far from here culturally as one can get.'

'So you ended it and got engaged again?' Again a complete lack of judgement in his voice, as if the night they had shared had never happened. As if the girl she was remembering had been a stranger. She moved in closer, enjoying his solid warmth. He put his arm around her and pulled her in tight. Minty rested her head on his shoulder, thankful for the tacit support.

'Well, yes,' she admitted, the familiar flush of guilt washing over her. Barty had been her first love; she'd just got in too deep. Remembering Spike made her feel like a fool. 'I was simply star-struck, I'm afraid. Spike was so famous and I loved his music; I couldn't believe he was interested in me. Of course, he was as old as Daddy. The two of them got on famously, all golf talk and "do you remember?" One day they both fell asleep after lunch and I couldn't tell which was which. It gave me quite a shock, and of course I realised it would never do. But then the papers decided I was just like my mother and that was that. I only have to smile at a man to be engaged to him, and there are all kinds of editorials warning him off me, and so-called psychologists analysing my past.'

'But you were hoping, third time lucky?'

The third. An ache squeezed her chest. 'Poor Joe,' she said. 'I'm such a disappointment.' A prickle of heat started behind her eyes, unfamiliar wetness. How glad she was of the darkness. 'I can put Bart and Spike down to immaturity, but I was old enough to know better with Joe. I should have known he wasn't for me the day he proposed on a ten-mile hike up a mountain.'

Luca gave a snort of amusement. 'I hope you were wearing sensible shoes.'

Minty elbowed him indignantly. 'Walking boots and a fleece, I'll have you know.'

Luca seemed to be shaking and when she turned to him she saw, with some surprise, that he was laughing. She had made people laugh at 'the tale of Minty's three fiancés' before, many times. But not like this.

'You wore a fleece?' he asked with some difficulty. 'Did it have an attached waterproof?'

'It was *practical*,' she said, then bit her lip, a bubble of amusement rising up inside her, dispersing the ache.

'You got engaged to a man who proposed to you in a fleece?'

'We were up a mountain!' But it was no use; the laughter that erupted from her wasn't self-deprecating, sarcastic, a disguise. It was real, all-consuming. He was right; it had been ridiculous.

'I think, *cara*, you had a lucky escape.' Minty's heart clenched at the endearment.

'From Joe? It wasn't all mountain-trekking; he liked pub quizzes as well.'

Luca laughed again, deep and sensual. 'From all of them. None of them were right for you.'

'Most people think *they* had a lucky escape from *me*.' Minty tried not to sound wistful.

'Most people,' he said, dropping a kiss onto the top of her head, 'are fools.'

CHAPTER EIGHT

'HUNGRY? WE COULD stop off in Siena for lunch.'

What did that mean? Did he want to stop off or would he rather get back? Minty shot Luca a quick glance. He was looking straight ahead, all his concentration on the road.

He had always been a careful driver, steady and sure, unwilling to take risks. She used to tease him about it but he had never allowed her to provoke him. Minty squirmed in her seat. She knew exactly how his parents had died and yet she had been thoughtless enough to laugh at Luca's driving. What a self-centred brat she had been.

Not that he had seemed to notice. It had driven her mad how easily he used to ignore her presence. Luca Di Tore, the golden boy, hard-working, courteous, who never put a foot wrong. Completely oblivious to her, to her need for his attention.

Getting him to notice her had been the main focus of most of Minty's summers. It had started out as a game, a way to annoy him and it had usually taken something fairly outrageous before he'd looked down from his lofty heights and deigned to bestow attention on her. It had been bad enough when she was small. By the time she was fourteen it had been unbearable.

She hadn't wanted to fancy Luca. But she had walked

in that summer and whoosh, bam, wallop, it had hit her hard. He had grown up whilst at university: grown up, grown out, grown hot. She'd barely been able to *breathe* when he was in the room, let alone say two words to him.

Of course, she would rather have been flayed alive than admit it even to herself, let alone anyone else. It was easier to act out even more, hide behind arrogance, insouciance and plain outrageousness.

It was a facade that had served her well for four years, right until Rose's funeral. And then she was too broken to hide. She had allowed Luca to see everything: her pain, her misery, her want, her need. And he had turned her away.

It had been utterly humiliating.

But last night she had allowed him in again, babbling on about Barty, about Joe, about rejections and *feelings*. Would she ever learn?

'So do you? Want lunch?' His voice was completely even. What was he thinking? Was he regretting the time they had spent together? Regretting *how* they'd spent their time?

'Define lunch.'

'Okay.' He sounded puzzled. 'A meal, in a restaurant, comprising at least two courses.'

'I didn't mean…' She paused. What did she mean? 'Is this a date? Or just lunch? What are we actually doing here?'

'Are you asking me what my intentions are?' Damn, he was laughing at her. Minty felt her teeth grinding together.

'Of course not!' Not exactly. 'I was just wondering what we're doing here. We spent all weekend together and back in Oschia we, well, we *were* together. And, if you hadn't noticed, at the moment we live together, work together... It's a little awkward.'

He didn't answer for a long moment as he negotiated the car around a tight bend. 'Minty, you're rebounding from an engagement. You're not ready for anything serious; I know that. Don't worry, I'm not planning to ask you to bear my four children.'

Obviously and, by the way, thank goodness. But it rankled a little how hilarious he found that idea.

'I thought we could just explore this thing, see where it takes us. Have some fun.' His voice sounded concerned. 'But if you want to stop, if you're feeling uncomfortable, then please just say.'

'No,' she said slowly. 'I'm fine.'

Fun. It was the answer she'd been hoping for, because of course he was right. She'd been engaged to another man just a few weeks ago—not that that had stopped Joe moving on, but Minty Davenport was not so fickle. At least, she was trying not to be.

So why did she feel disappointed? It was her stupid fourteen-year-old self with a house-sized crush and a romantic streak longer than the Arno. Three engagements should have dried that streak right out.

Luca was right. Why plan? They both knew this would burn out eventually. They were so different, wanted such different things. Why spoil the moment with labels and definitions? That was far more Luca's style than hers—if he could be relaxed, then of course she could be too!

'You're right,' she said, leaning back, forcing herself to sound unconcerned. 'Lunch sounds lovely.'

'Admit it, the view's gorgeous.' Minty waved her soup spoon at him. 'The soup's good too.'

'The soup is four times as expensive as it would have been round the corner.' Luca shook his head. 'Hope the view's worth it.'

They were sat at a table in Siena's bustling main square. A place fit only for tourists, Luca had told her.

'I never mind paying for a view,' Minty said, gesturing around with her spoon. 'I'd rather sit in St Mark's Square or enjoy a view of the Pantheon with my coffee than save a couple of euros and sit in an alleyway somewhere, looking at damp brickwork.'

'It can be a lot more than a couple of euros.' Luca shook his head. She had no idea how privileged she was. Even Luca, who had grown up in comfortable surroundings, ran a very profitable business, travelled first class and wore tailor-made suits balked at the mark-up in these places. 'Not everyone can afford to spend ten euros on a coffee.'

Minty didn't respond for a few moments, concentrating on her soup. When she spoke, her voice was low. 'Joe always said I was spoilt.' She tried to laugh if off but there was no humour in it and Luca was aware of a most uncharacteristic urge to search out Joe and force him to apologise.

With his fists, if need be.

No man should have the power to make those bright eyes so dim, to make a confident, laughing girl so full of self-doubt.

The man was undoubtedly a fool. He said so, but Minty shook her head.

'Funny, isn't it, how the things some people like in you are the things somebody else despises? Spike loved all that—the trust fund and ancestors who fought for Charles I and advised Henry VIII. Barty took it for granted because that was his world too. Joe, on the other

hand...' She shook her head. 'It wasn't just my ances-
try, it was the money too—especially as I didn't earn
it. We always had to travel budget airlines and stay in
youth hostels. It was fun at first.'

She looked up and smiled at Luca. 'It's always fun
to try something new. But I wanted to treat him for his
birthday so I took him to New York. First class, a lovely
hotel and the latest must-go-to restaurant. It *was* outra-
geously expensive, to be honest, even I thought so, but
he sulked for the whole of the holiday. I wasn't behav-
ing the way he expected me to behave. Apparently I was
the one who was meant to compromise all the time. We
split up a week later.'

She went back to her soup. Luca sat back in his chair
and watched her for a moment. Her face, what he could
see of it under those ridiculously large sunglasses, was
unconcerned but he was beginning to understand her.
He chose his words carefully. 'Compromise is important, but on both sides, Minty. If someone can't accept
you for who you are, love everything about you, even
the bits that are harder to take, then they're not right
for you.'

She pushed her soup bowl away and looked up, a
bright smile plastered onto her face. 'That's the fairy
tale, isn't it? The dream we're sold: someone will fall
for you flaws and all.' She shook her head vehemently.
'I don't think so. I think everyone has to pretend a little, suppress themselves a little, if they want it to last.'

Minty reached out for the bread and tore a piece off
it. 'Or be alone. Look at my Great-great-aunt Prudence.
No man of the time wanted an Amazon explorer for a
wife; she chose adventure over settling down and never
regretted it.'

Luca visualised a turn-of-the-century Minty, hair

streaming behind her, one hand on a large straw hat as the paddle boat pulled out into piranha-infested waters. 'I don't agree,' he said carefully. 'I think it's possible to find someone who complements you, a true partner. Someone who supports whatever you want to do, even if you want to sail down the Amazon!'

Minty shook her head. She was toying with her bread, tearing off small bits of the chewy inside and rolling it around in her hands. Luca watched her long fingers so busily at work, so unsettled. 'Love is fun for a little while, but I don't think it forms a good basis for "for ever". There's too much pretence, too much compromising to make it work. Mutual respect, that's the key; a sensible arrangement so you know what you're getting up front. And then no need to change—or to keep moving on.'

Like the marriage Luca was hoping for. Suddenly it didn't sound so appealing. It sounded cold, clinical. What did he plan? A dating agency? An advert? Arrogantly he had just sort of assumed that he would just need to look around. After all, he was successful; he had a nice house, a business.

All his own hair.

A flush of mortification spread through him. Did he really think a list of desirable attributes was all that was needed? Was he really so conceited he thought he'd just have to click his fingers and a queue of suitable wives would form?

And what made him think that finding someone who fulfilled a checklist would make him happy anyway? After all, his sophisticated, city-bred, society mother had been happy with her countrified husband.

'Don't give up,' he said. 'Someone out there would give up everything to travel along the Amazon with you.'

'For a while, maybe.' Her voice trailed off, the heap of small balls of bread on her plate growing larger. Luca opened his mouth to reassure her, to press the point home. But he didn't know what to say.

At that moment the waiter brought out large plates heaped with steaming pasta, covered with a delicious-smelling tomato and vegetable sauce garnished with anchovies.

'Good, they haven't stinted on the anchovies,' Minty said enthusiastically, picking up her fork. 'I love them.'

And the moment was gone. But he wanted to hold on to it, hold on to her. Spend more time in her world, her impulsive, irresponsible, fun world, away from the everyday cares and stresses he had been shouldering for as long as he could remember.

Be someone else, someone she wanted, for just a little bit longer.

'We don't have to go straight back to Oschia.'

Minty looked up from the car's state-of-the-art and ridiculously complicated stereo. 'I thought we were getting to the stage where all we would have to do was think of a tune and it would miraculously play,' she grumbled. 'I don't understand what it wants me to do.'

Luca reached down without looking and one second later the strains of classical music filled the car. It was a violin solo and Minty was immediately transported back to the night before. To that moment of sheer perfection and happiness.

'Too solemn,' she said hurriedly. 'I want something poppy.' Something that wasn't going to evoke any embarrassing memories of weakness. Of neediness.

Luca obligingly changed the music until he reached

a well-known female singer-songwriter and Minty nodded approvingly. 'Perfect,' she said, leaning back and
putting her bare feet back on the dashboard, throwing
a provocative glance at Luca as she did so. She knew
how much it annoyed him.

She wiggled her toes.

'So?' he prompted.

'So?'

'What do you think about not heading back?'

'We already stopped off for lunch,' Minty pointed
out, regarding her toenails critically. She had painted
them silver for the party but they were already chip-
ping. Maybe something bright and cheerful next; she
had bought a vivid orange in Florence which might do.
She slid a glance over at Luca. He probably wouldn't
really appreciate her painting her nails in his car.

He was a smooth driver, though.

And at that thought a mental image of the two of
them the day before, entwined, filled her head. She
squirmed in her seat. Driving wasn't the only thing he
did smoothly.

'I didn't mean for an hour or two. I meant for a few
days. After all...' His head jerked meaningfully to the
three large suitcases in the boot. 'You have enough there
to last an apocalyptic catastrophe.'

She hadn't brought that much with her. Minty
glanced into the back. Oh, the man had a point.

'Won't people talk?'

He shrugged. 'Who? The tabloids don't even know
who I am.'

'Not people—*people*,' she said. 'Your family. Our—
your—colleagues.'

He looked over at her, disbelief written clearly on
his face. 'We have been living together since you got

here and have just spent a weekend together—with my uptight, old-fashioned grandfather—being photographed at a very public charity event. They are already talking. Let's clear off and let the fuss die down. If we're lucky, Andreo in accounts will finally ask Maria on reception out and we will be forgotten. Yesterday's news.'

Doubt gnawed at Minty's stomach. On one hand, they were having a good time. He was funny, easy to talk to, good in bed. On the other, she risked exposing him to the crazy media circus that was her life. He might shrug off a few gossip websites but would he be so sanguine when an ex sold her story to a newspaper? When it was his front door the photographers surrounded?

'What about work?' she said instead, watching him carefully. He gave nothing away, his expression bland.

'I'm quite happy to authorise your leave. Come on, Minty, I'm talking about a road trip—just a few days.'

'Hmm…' It wasn't going away with Luca that worried her, it was coming back. The longer she spent with him, the more under a spell she was, like Sleeping Beauty in a dream world of warm sun, olive trees and a handsome ice-cream tycoon. The difference was that Sleeping Beauty had woken up to her happy-ever-after; Minty would wake up to the dullness of everyday life. There would be no one to hack through the forest of thorns and rescue her; she would have to do it herself.

Again.

The longer she stayed with Luca, the harder it would be to fight her way back into the real world.

Last time she'd rebounded into a disastrous series of relationships after just one night. A night that had left her aching with unconsummated desire, feeling all alone. What was she thinking, spending all this time with him, letting him get so close?

But maybe this would work the other way. She fancied him; that was pretty undeniable. But he wasn't irresistibly perfect. Sure, *now* he was suddenly all about the impulsive days off work, the long walks, the sudden holidays, but at heart he was still the disapproving, sensible, solid Luca. He couldn't keep that side of himself locked away for too long. And when that side resurrected itself he'd blame her for leading him astray. Just like he always had.

Maybe she needed this finally to move on. To let the crush play itself out until the scales fell irrevocably from her eyes. They would. They always did.

And she'd be free.

'Minty.' His voice was caramel and cream, a hint of something darker, more intoxicating threaded through it. 'Don't overthink this.'

'Normally people *tell* me to think before I act,' she pointed out. 'Here I am, trying for a new responsible me, and you're holding up a perfect-looking apple and telling me how how juicy it is!' The problem was, she wasn't very good at resisting temptation, and they didn't come much more tempting than the tall Italian beside her. She sighed. Would a short trip really hurt? She could be careful; careful not to get pulled into his world, careful to be herself, to stay flighty and silly and impulsive.

'I am supposed to be doing the consumer focus groups this week.' But she allowed her voice to lack conviction. She slid a provocative glance at him through her eyelashes and she saw him smile.

'Alessandro can do that.' The smile was in his voice and a rush of heat flooded through her. It wasn't fair;

JESSICA GILMORE 127

how could someone's voice have this effect on her? This man's voice...

'You may get tired of me without the office to escape to. I can be very demanding.'

'That,' he said, looking directly at her, the heat in his eyes making her gasp, 'I am counting on.'

'Where do you want to go?' Her voice wasn't quite steady. His proximity, the way his eyes seemed to strip and caress her, were making it hard for her to remain cool. In control.

'Roma?' He didn't sound so certain. Minty knew with utter certainty it was the last place he wanted to go, but that he knew she'd enjoy it. The squeeze in her chest was almost suffocating. It wasn't often that anyone put her interests before their own.

'What if I wanted to have a beer overlooking the Pantheon?'

'Then you would pay.' His mouth lifted with a triumphant smirk. 'I'll warn you, mine will be a large one. Plus some kind of bar snack or two.'

'Shop?'

A small pause; she peeped at him through her lashes. He looked amused. 'Please just wear sensible shoes and don't expect me to carry all your bags.'

'Sensible and pretty,' Minty assured him. 'But I don't want to go to Rome.'

An eyebrow quirked. 'No? Then where shall I head to? North to the lakes or the mountains? Or I could drive us to Venice or Verona?'

Verona was new territory; the lakes were always lovely. Venice? Suddenly the thought of a jostling, crowded city didn't seem that appealing, even one as quirkily beautiful as Venice.

Besides, Luca would hate it.

Minty looked out at the sunshine and thought about the light and very spring-like clothing she had just purchased. It was still early in the season. 'I think we should go south,' she decided.

Luca's eyes flickered to her bare legs and feet, and he grinned but didn't say anything.

'Are you sure?' Minty wasn't sure what she was asking. Was he sure about taking the time off, about taking a trip with her? About being with her?

'Completely. I haven't taken any time off in well over a year. A break will probably do me good.'

'Okay.' She bit down on her bottom lip. These doubts were ridiculous. Luca was a grown man, a responsible, sensible CEO. If he said he wanted to take some time off, then it wasn't her job to question him or dissuade him.

It was just that impulsive road trips were more her style than his. She wasn't used to people adapting to her ways.

Minty slouched down further into her seat, deliberately, provocatively, assuming an almost horizontal, ultra-relaxed position. 'South it is. How far are we going to go? All the way?' She allowed a touch of innuendo to enter her voice and was gratified to see him swallow, his jaw clench. His knuckles whitened on the steering wheel.

'There probably isn't time to get to Sicily and to enjoy it properly. Not if we're going to drive—unless you want to fly?'

'Oh, we are definitely driving. A road trip is much more fun if it actually involves a road,' she insisted. 'Flying makes it a mini-break; not the same thing at all.'

'I went on holiday to Sorrento with my parents the year before they died,' Luca offered. His face was blank, expressionless, but for all the studied nonchalance there was a dark undercurrent in his voice. 'I never wanted to go back before—too many memories, I suppose—but maybe it's time to make some new ones. Of course, you've probably been there far too many times.'

Minty shook her head. 'Not even once,' she said promptly. 'Sorrento it is. Capri, Amalfi, Positano—sounds like a socialite's dream. I bet I can find us a café where the price of coffee will make you cry.'

'I can't wait,' Luca murmured drily, but he reached over with one hand and touched her, just a fleeting caress of her knee, yet it was as if a flame had scorched her, the heat travelling across her body. Minty resisted the urge to grab his hand, to move it back.

'I've always wanted to visit Pompeii,' she said instead, dragging her eyes away from the strong, capable hands handling the steering wheel with such deft assurance. 'Of course I'll deny it, claim that you forced me to go.'

'Dragged you there kicking and screaming,' he agreed. 'And marched you up Vesuvius at gun-point.'

'Naturally. After all, volcano climbing is so nineteenth-century, darling. That terribly vulgar Hamilton woman.'

Despite her earlier doubts, a surge of excitement began to build up inside Minty. A new place, a new adventure; sun, sea, culture and stunning scenery.

And, best of all, she was free. There were no expectations from the man next to her, no promises he would end up breaking. He knew as well as she did that this was a moment out of time, that they would resume their real lives at some point.

She just hoped that it wouldn't hurt her too much when they did.

CHAPTER NINE

'WHAT ARE YOU PLANNING?' Minty rolled on top of Luca, holding his wrists prisoner in her hands. 'I'm not letting you go until you tell me.'

'In that case, you'll never know,' Luca promised her.

She changed tack, dropping feather-light kisses along his jaw, nibbling tantalisingly at the corner of his mouth. 'Tell me,' she whispered.

He moved slightly, fitting comfortably under her, angling his face so that he could capture her mouth with his. The sweetness was a heady rush. The man was addictive.

'It's a surprise, which means you don't get to find out until we do it,' he murmured against her mouth.

Minty's only response was to press deeper, harder into the kiss, her hands still loosely encircling his wrists. Her breasts pressed tightly against his chest, her legs wrapping round his as she relinquished control, soft and pliant against his mouth. She felt good, wrapped around him; she fit perfectly.

She pulled back, hazy with desire. 'I hate surprises.'

With one movement he flipped her round, freeing his wrists as he in turn captured hers, smiling down at her indignant face. 'Good things come to those who wait. You, *cara*, wait here. Dress.' He glanced out of the window at the picture-perfect blue sky then back at Minty, rumpled in a vest top and little cotton shorts. 'Actually, stay as you are. You're perfect. But pack a bikini and a jumper for later.' He leant over, grazed her mouth with his. 'I'll see you downstairs in thirty minutes. Oh, and Minty? No fleeces or walking boots required.'

Minty grabbed one of the many pillows off the large bed and threw it at his head, scrabbling around for another to use as a defence as he deftly caught it and threw it back with unerring aim. By the time she had recovered he was gone, off to organise whatever surprise he had planned.

Normally surprises made Minty nervous. They involved moonlight, rings, promises: promises the maker never kept.

She was pretty sure that Luca didn't have a proposal planned. They hadn't spoken one word about the future, had spent the past week living in the here and now, but she knew what he wanted long term.

A wife and children. A home.

Did he see her in that role? Minty was too afraid to ask. She didn't know what would be worse, a yes or a no. Because she knew all too well that she wasn't what Luca needed in the long term, no matter how seductive a future with him was.

She was good for day trips and weekends away, for making a man feel good about himself, but she wasn't a long-term prospect. Three men had made that all too clear; she wouldn't let Luca hammer the point home.

Every time she'd thought that this was the one, the man, the future that was right for her. She believed her own dreams. Her own drama.

But reality always intruded, always proved her wrong.

She just wished this ridiculous crush would hurry

up and be over. If only spending time with Luca wasn't proving to be so much fun. Hopefully his surprise would misfire terribly and be the wake-up call she needed.

Because so far the holiday had been ridiculously perfect, from the small boutique hotel, high in the hills overlooking the Bay of Naples, to the company. Luca had been amusing, interesting, knowledgeable, insightful. He hadn't been stuffy once. It was almost disappointing.

With a sigh Minty rolled over and stared down at the crisp, white bedspread, scenes from the previous week playing in her mind. It was difficult to pick one day out; they had all been amazing.

There had been the first day, wandering hand in hand around Pompeii in respectful silence as they'd stood in front of the burned remains of terrified Romans trying to escape the ashes raining down on them from above. The less respectful and all too obvious jokes as they'd looked at the 'menu' in the ancient brothel.

The next afternoon they'd hiked up the steep trail that wound round Mount Vesuvius, peering into the covered, smoking crater before returning to a local restaurant to sample wine made from grapes grown on the deadly, dusty slopes.

Yesterday they had taken the small hovercraft over to Capri, walking the hilly path to the remains of Tiberius's villa, imagining the screams of long-dead slaves thrown onto the rocks below, before returning to fashionable, frothy Capri town for what did end up being the most expensive coffee Luca had ever drunk. Minty had paid; it had been a point of pride.

And unlike Joe he had accepted gracefully, allowing her to treat him. Minty glared at the bedspread resentfully; she had counted on a ridiculous argument over paying.

Last night she had accepted his laughing challenge and proved that, yes, she could manage an entire traditional Italian meal, starting off with a plate of fried fish of every description before moving on to pasta, and then chicken served with vegetables and small fried potatoes. She had eaten every morsel and then, as they'd wandered round the town for the evening promenade, she had demanded *gelato.*

Her stomach had felt a little sore for a few hours afterwards but the victory had been sweet.

And then there were the nights and the long, lazy mornings, totally unforgettable—not just for the way they'd explored each other's bodies, although that was undeniably amazing. Minty's whole body began to heat up at the memories; there was nothing safe or boring about Luca's lovemaking. But it was about more than sex, even the best sex Minty had ever experienced. It was about the comfortable silences, the meaningless conversations which, by their very inanity, were intimate.

The holiday had been utterly perfect.

Minty groaned. She liked to win but when it came to getting over Luca Di Tore she had to admit that right now she was failing. Failing badly. And the consequences of failure were far too high.

Her heart, her already fragile sense of self-worth, were sitting in his hand waiting to be carefully crushed unless she could find a way to extricate herself from this situation, keeping her mind and her job as she did so.

She might pride herself on her resourcefulness but right now Minty had to admit she was completely and utterly clueless. She was in danger of losing her heart, of losing everything.

Tomorrow they would be back in Oschia. She'd enjoy this last day for all she was worth because once they got back she needed to put the brakes on. Before it was too late.

Minty was uncharacteristically punctual, appearing in the car park exactly thirty minutes after Luca had left her, dressed, if not in the rumpled short pyjamas he had suggested she wear, in denim cut-offs of a similar style and a vest top that clearly showed off the ties of her bikini top. A large bag was slung over her shoulder crammed so full that Luca could see a towel, a magazine and a rolled-up white shirt spilling out of the top.

'Are you sure you have everything?' he asked, taking the bag from her, mock-staggering under the weight.

'If I don't know where we're going or what we're doing how can I pack lightly?' she retorted. 'What if we are going to a fancy restaurant, or scuba diving, or touring the area's ice-cream factories? I just like to be prepared.'

'That you are,' Luca assured her as he rifled through the bag to find flip-flops, a sundress, hairbrush, her make-up bag, a jumper and a large floppy hat. That was just the top layer. He wasn't sure what was underneath. It could be anything.

'So?' Minty demanded. 'Where are we going?' She began walking towards the car but Luca put a hand on her shoulders and steered her round, away from his own black four-by-four to a red vintage Ferrari convertible parked by the hotel's gates.

'Your chariot, *signorina*,' he said, opening the passenger door and ushering her into the cracked leather seat.

'Luca, this isn't a shorts and top car, this is a frock

and headscarf car. I'm completely underdressed for it,' Minty protested, running her hands in awe over the chrome finish on the polished wood dashboard.

'This isn't actually the surprise,' he said. 'It's just transport to the surprise.' He grinned at her as he walked round to the driver's side and slid into the low-slung seat. 'I'm aware that you find my car a little staid in these glamorous surroundings.'

'No, not at all,' she said. 'Honestly, I love your car; it's very solid, very safe.'

His mouth twisted wryly. 'Solid and safe like me, but not glamorous like you. I thought you might appreciate a bit of glamour.'

'I'm hardly glamorous right now,' Minty said, laughing, looking down at her denim shorts. Luca's eyes followed her gaze and travelled further down the long, bare legs, no longer pale but slightly tanned to a light honey colour. 'And you are not just solid and safe. In fact, I'd say not safe at all.' She leant over to press a kiss into his neck, right on his pulse. He felt the imprint burning as she moved away. 'I love the car, though. Is this really not the full surprise?'

'Wait and see,' he said. 'Just enjoy the ride.'

The car was in fantastic condition for its age and a joy to handle. It felt so light and insubstantial under Luca's control, much like its passenger reclining back in comfort, enormous sunglasses obscuring half her face, hair whipping around in the wind. Luca was so used to the weight and bulk of his car—he had only driven large, sturdy cars—that the freedom and flexibility of the convertible was both alarming and intoxicating.

Again, much like his passenger.

It wasn't far to their destination. For a moment Luca wished he had decided to drive all the way and keep the car for the day, had trusted himself to navigate something so flimsy around the famously tortuous hairpin bends of the Amalfi coastal road. After all, no vehicle was completely safe. When he had begun driving he'd researched hard, ensured he'd bought the safest car possible. If driving a tank had been a viable option, then he would gladly have done it. Maybe he should have pushed through those barriers sooner, learnt to relax and let go sooner.

There were definitely some upsides to spontaneity, although planning ahead had its uses too, in pleasure as well as business. Today, for instance, had been meticulously planned and kept secret. He was well aware it was driving Minty mad.

All too soon he was pulling up in the small car park adjoining the harbour jutting out from Sorrento's rocky coastline. Minty pouted in disappointment. 'That was quick; I was wanting more of a ride.' It had to be deliberate, the innuendo in her voice.

Luca slid an arm round her slender frame, enjoying the familiarity of her skin under his. He pulled her close, lifting her chin with his other hand, dropping a long kiss onto the provocatively full mouth. 'Patience,' he whispered against her ear. 'The ride isn't over yet.'

Opening his door, Luca strolled round to the other side of the car and, with exaggerated gallantry, assisted Minty out of the vehicle. After a last, longing look at the car, Minty allowed him to lead her up to the harbour.

'It can't be Capri, we've been there. Ischia? One of the spas there? I can just see you in a mud bath having your feet nibbled by fish. Oh, *eugh*; not a fishing trip, I hope?' Luca didn't bat an eyelid as Minty fished for information but continued along the harbour path until he found the berth he was looking for.

'Ladies first,' he said, gesturing towards the small gangplank which led aboard the smart cabin cruiser moored there. Minty stopped, one hand on the rail, pushed her sunglasses up her head and regarded him suspiciously. 'No fishing?' she asked.

'Not a rod in sight,' he promised.

He followed Minty on board where she immediately began exploring, her voice full of excitement as she called out each new discovery. On deck there were comfortable seats both in the glass-covered steering cabin and the open back. A door led down to a large, comfortable cabin with a tiny galley kitchen, small but inclusive shower room and a seating area. Minty opened another door and raised an eyebrow at the immaculately made-up bed. 'Mr Di Tore, I am beginning to suspect you of dishonourable intentions,' she murmured.

'Always,' he said, lifting up the heavy fall of hair and kissing the back of her neck, heat fizzing through his veins as she leant against him, submitting to the caress. 'But not yet. I would like to be somewhere just a little more private when I show you just how dishonourable I can be.'

He felt her shiver against him; moving away was exquisite torture.

'Do you know how to drive this thing?' She followed him out on deck.

'*Sail*, and yes. My father was a keen sailor. Funny for a man of the land, I suppose, but every holiday we spent on or near the sea. He taught me to handle one of these when I was eight.'

'You *have* handled one since?'

'Relax, Minty, I know what I'm doing. Besides, you crewed halfway round the world; I'm sure you could cope if I need you.'

'I was more of a galley hand,' Minty admitted. 'Besides, that involved sails and ropes and swabbing. This all looks a little more technical.' Her eyes fell to the control panel.

'Luckily, then, all you need to do is sunbathe and relax,' Luca told her. 'Okay, are you ready?'

'Aye aye, captain.' Minty saluted smartly as she folded herself into the seat beside Luca. He turned the key, switched on the engine and felt the motor purr into life. They were off.

Minty was clearly in her element. Luca had barely navigated the boat out of the dock but she was already stripped to her bikini, lying prostrate on the comfortable lounger laid out ready for her. She looked like a sun goddess, all golden hair and skin, worshipping the warmth. And like any goddess there was an element of wildness, of danger and unpredictability.

Luca hadn't brought Minty here to tame her; he hadn't expected this holiday to have any long-term results. He just wanted to relax for the first time in a really long time, with the one person who made him forget his cares, his responsibilities.

But he didn't feel so relaxed now. The holiday was coming to an end and, for all his talk about having fun and no expectations, things had changed. It felt more intense.

But how did you tame a wild thing without damaging something essential inside it? She wanted him now— that was all too clear—and she might still want him tomorrow. But the day after that, when she got bored with the Italian countryside and her role at Di Tore Dolce?

It would be safer, better, to put an end to whatever this was, to get his life back on track.

The problem was Luca was beginning to like walking on the wild side just a little too much. He didn't know if he could go back even if he wanted to. And right now he really didn't.

Minty stretched out luxuriously. 'That was amazing, thank you.' She cast a last regretful look at the remains of their feast: olives, little ciabatta rolls, cured meats, cheese, anchovies and a whole host of salads and cold roasted vegetables.

No, not one more olive... Although, she might have just a little bit of room... She eyed Luca plaintively, making sure she had her best puppy-dog eyes. 'Is there pudding?'

Luca stared at her. 'Pudding?' He sounded incredulous as he waved at the meagre remains of the picnic. 'You really have room?'

Minty considered his question for a moment. She was full, sure, but there was definitely room for a nice, creamy zabaglione, or even a panna cotta. Possibly tiramisu, if it wasn't too rich. 'Just a little.'

He shook his head, amusement crinkling the corners of his eyes. 'You ate at least four rolls at breakfast and a big bowl of fruit.'

'Fruit doesn't count!'

'Then there was the lemon cake in Positano.'

'She said it was a speciality. It would have been rude not to.'

'Pizza in Amalfi.'

'Very thin base, and I had a rocket salad with it.'

'*Gelato* in Ravello.'

'*That* was research.'

'Where do you put it all?' The amber eyes raked her long frame appreciatively. Minty sighed, rolling over onto her back and massaging her full tummy.

'Good metabolism, I suppose. Besides, you had as much and more, and I'm not teasing you. You *have* got pudding; I know you have.'

Luca didn't answer for a moment. He just lay there watching her, an annoying twinkle in his eye, and Minty clenched her hands together, the urge to break his smug stillness, throw a roll at him, strong.

It wasn't dusk yet but it wasn't far off, the light beginning to dim, the sea darkening to a deep navy. They weren't far out, the lights of Sorrento clearly visible in the distance. Soon they would have to return the boat to shore, climb back into the vintage convertible and drive back to the hotel for their last night there. Tomorrow they would return to their ordinary world.

How were they going to navigate working together, living together, after this? She pushed the thought away. There was time enough tomorrow to worry about tomorrow, she told herself. *Enjoy this.*

It might be the last time.

'I may have something else,' Luca admitted. 'But I thought you might enjoy it with a glass of Prosecco, and for that I need us to be moored. No drinking and sailing.'

Minty's face fell. 'It's so peaceful out here.'

'Which is why we're mooring at a tiny harbour south of Sorrento. No one else will be there. I thought we could spend the night there.' His eyes gleamed gold. 'Test that bed out. Tomorrow morning, we'll just sail back to Sorrento, drive back to the hotel and check out.'

'Perfect,' Minty said, ignoring the tight squeeze in her chest at the thought of returning. 'I'll just…' She gestured at the remains of the meal. 'I needed a moment alone.

She didn't know why the thought of returning was

affecting her so much. After all, all road trips—and boat trips—had to come to an end.

She just didn't know where her destination was. Or, worse, she didn't know where she wanted it to be.

Safely moored at the tiny harbour, shielded from the rocks that dominated the dramatic coastline, protected from the night traffic crossing the sea, they sat out on the deck staring out to sea at the stars shining with such fierce intensity above them. Both were lost in their own worlds.

A glass of chilled Prosecco, fresh raspberries and a trio of puddings were laid out on the table. Minty took a sip, enjoying the tart fizz on her tongue, and eyed the three puddings. Perfect: lemon tart, panna cotta and a rich tiramisu. Why choose? A mouthful—or two—of each would be far more enjoyable.

Pudding was like life—better with variety.

Luca was tapping away on his laptop, pausing every now and then to fork a spoonful of tart into his mouth. He had barely worked since they had arrived in Sorrento, even switching his phone off—or to mute, at least—some days. Their impending return was obviously affecting him as well, as he was slowly returning to the real world. He must have sensed Minty's gaze on him and he looked up and smiled.

'I'm sorry, just a few instructions for Marco before he leaves tomorrow. Then I am all yours, I promise.'

'You better be.' But she wasn't upset or offended. She was happy just to sit back and soak in the sea air, looking out at the stars.

Her own phone buzzed and she picked it up, scrolling through to the message. Her father. She didn't want to open it, to let his disapproval taint the perfection of this last night, but neither did she want to spend the evening worrying about what it might say.

'What's wrong?'

The concern in Luca's voice wrapped around her like a heavy velvet cloak. It was nice to hear. As long as she remembered not to get too used to it.

'Just Daddy dearest,' she said, keeping her tone as light as she could.

'What does he want?'

'Probably to tell me off for something. Or to send a picture of the heir, spare or girl achieving something amazing, like first place in a finger-painting contest.'

'You're not close to your brothers and sister?'

'They're young enough to be my niece and nephews,' Minty pointed out. 'Plus, I am officially a bad influence, so Stepmama prefers I stay away as much as possible. It's funny; when I was a child I longed for siblings. Now I have three and I know nothing about them. Apart from their genius at finger-painting, that is.'

She stared moodily at the phone. Damn her father. He'd cut her off from her inheritance and her family. What right did he have to intrude on her evening? He'd made it clear she had no place in his life, so he should just stay out of hers.

Luca was looking at her intently, his golden gaze drilling through all her carefully erected barriers. 'Did your mother have any more children?'

'And ruin her figure?' There was no pretence at lightness now. Minty could feel twenty years of carefully buried bitterness and betrayal rising to the surface. 'Children are terribly aging, Luca dearest. She stopped inviting me over when I turned fourteen; it's hard to keep knocking decades off your age with a five-foot-eleven daughter standing there.'

'I'm sorry.' He didn't try to touch her or comfort her and she was oddly relieved that he just let her talk.

Minty brushed away an angry tear she hadn't even felt forming. 'If it weren't for Rose and Gio, I wouldn't have had any kind of family. Once the divorce was finalised, my parents seemed to think they'd dissolved any tie to me as well. One minute I was the pampered child of London's most glamorous couple, the next I was sat in the headmistress's office while she phoned around trying to find someone to come and collect me for Christmas.'

Sometimes in her nightmares she was transported back there: empty, echoing halls smelling of polish; swinging her legs on a tall, straight-backed wooden chair, staring at the doors, waiting for someone to rush in with explanations, reasons for their lateness. To reassure her that she hadn't been forgotten.

Only they never came.

'I was seven.' She spoke so quietly she didn't know if Luca had heard her.

Luca shook his head, his eyes full of sympathy. 'I'm sorry I wasn't more aware back then, more help. Of course, I knew you weren't close to your parents, but when you first showed up I was too bound up in my own grief to find out why you spent your summers with us. I was too resentful of you, not understanding enough.'

'That's not true,' Minty protested, turning to face him, admiring the strongly cut features silhouetted against the dark sea behind him, against the moon hanging low in the sky. 'I was a complete brat. I know that. I meant to be. If you're always in trouble, *someone* has to pay attention; I learnt that lesson all too well. Besides, you'd lost your parents. You shouldn't have had to make allowances for me.'

'Rose asked me to,' he said simply. 'She gave up her life in London and moved to a different country to look after her husband's nephew. I should have listened to her.'

Minty felt a tingle of warmth; someone *had* cared about her. 'It's a shame she didn't have children of her own. She'd have made a perfect mother.' She couldn't remember a time when she hadn't wished that Rose was really her mother and had weaved elaborate, romantic tales of kidnapping and evil witches.

'They wanted them but it didn't happen. She told me once that she wasn't sad about it, that you and I were the children of her heart.'

Minty snuggled further into the reassuring solidity of Luca's embrace, rubbing her cheek against the soft wool of the cashmere jumper he'd pulled on as the coolness of the evening set in. Talking about Rose reminded her of the worry she felt every time she saw Gio. 'I wish she was still here. Which reminds me, is Gio all right? He seems…' She struggled for the right words. 'He seems lost.'

'He still misses Rose.'

'We all do. But it's been six years, Luca.'

'It's different for him. We loved her and grieve for her but we have our lives. She *was* his life.'

'But he used to be so busy,' Minty argued. 'Now he doesn't come into work any more, not outside of board meetings. He doesn't cook or go walking or play tennis. He just sits there, watching TV. There must be something we can do, some way to help him. What have you tried in the past?'

She was so earnest, so ready to help, her own pain pushed aside in her concern for Gio's welfare. A hot flush of shame engulfed Luca, heating his cheeks despite the coolness of the evening. How could he explain to her? How could he admit that he hadn't been there for his uncle when he'd needed him? That once again he had let down someone he cared about, someone he loved? That over time the chasm between them had widened so much, Luca wasn't sure he *could* reach him any more?

'You weren't here.' It was the wrong thing to say, he knew that straight away. He felt her withdraw physically, withdraw emotionally.

But it was true, she hadn't been there; she had run away, left the man who had effectively raised her alone in his grief. Left Luca.

'I was hurt, confused.'

'So was I!' The outburst shocked Luca as much as it evidently shocked Minty. She was on her feet, back against the cabin door, the light from the cabin highlighting the surprise in her eyes. Luca took a deep breath. This night was supposed to be about fun, about the two of them. It wasn't about dragging up the past.

'That's the point, Minty. We all grieved alone, and by the time I realised what a mess Gio was in it was too late. We were fractured as a family the second Rose died. I blame myself.'

He did, entirely. Every time he saw Gio, he felt the same stab of guilt.

'I should have seen what was happening, that he was sinking, but I was too busy wallowing myself. Missing Rose, feeling guilty over what happened with you, angry with you, angry with myself. I failed Gio, just as I failed my parents.'

As he said the words it was like releasing a heavy burden off his shoulders, off his heart. He hadn't even realised that he was equating the two tragedies, that he had bound his grief, guilt and anger over both losses together.

Minty's eyes softened and her stance became less defensive, although she remained beyond his reach. 'How can any of this be your fault?' she asked. 'Your parents died in a car accident. Rose was ill. None of it had anything to do with you.'

Nothing to do with him? If only that were true. 'Did you know that only the front of the car was crushed?' he asked. Minty shook her head mutely. 'I was supposed to be with them that day, but I begged and pleaded to spend the day with a friend instead. If I'd been less selfish, if I'd been there, I might have wriggled out of the car. I could have got help earlier, maybe freed them. The policeman said that they didn't die straight away.'

It haunted him, thinking of them crushed, injured, dying. That he might have saved them. That he *could* have saved them.

Minty's eyes were fixed on Luca, her voice soft but clear, matter of fact, reaching through the guilt and anger. 'You were eleven. You might have died yourself. If they were conscious—and they were unlikely to be, Luca—they must have been so glad that you weren't there, that you were safe.'

'I could have saved them,' Luca said, but his tone lacked conviction.

'No, you couldn't have.' She took his face in her hands, her palms soft and cool against his face. 'You were just a boy then. But now you're a man, a ridiculously sexy, successful man, who feels like he has to save the world. You know, Luca, the world doesn't need saving. But Gio does. And you can reach him. You might be the only person who can.'

'Will you help me?' His chest constricted while he waited for her answer. He needed her for this, as he had needed her back then. He needed what remained of their strange family of lonely, damaged people bound together by history, by blood, by love for one remarkable woman.

'Of course.' And just like that he could breathe again. 'Start now, Luca. I'm going to go and change, see what my father wanted. You call Gio. Talk to him properly. Invite him over for dinner tomorrow night. I'll be here waiting. I'll be right here.'

She released his face and bent over to press a light butterfly kiss on his forehead and, after one last searching look into his eyes, turned round and disappeared back into the cabin. Luca pulled his phone out of his pocket. She was right. It was time to move on. Time to let go of the anger, the guilt and the pain. Time to put the past behind them.

It was time to be a family again, and this time Minty was right here with him. Right where she belonged.

CHAPTER TEN

MINTY SWALLOWED NERVOUSLY and smoothed down her hair for the tenth time in as many minutes, adjusting the hem of her dress. Another carefully chosen outfit for another board meeting, another presentation.

Only, this one was different. This time she had the CEO's support.

Looking down the length of the table, she locked on to his gaze for a moment. Desire shivered down her spine at the molten heat blazing in his eyes: lust; pride; affection. A heady combination.

Gio was also at the table. It was only a few weeks since he had come to dinner, just a few weeks since a long, frank, cathartic conversation that had gone on long into the night. He still wasn't the Gio she remembered—she wasn't sure he ever would be—but there was a marked improvement. Regular meals at the house, including him in business decisions and trips out, making him part of the family, were already having a positive effect.

Family... Funny how she'd spent her life mourning the disintegration of hers, yet had never realised that she'd created a new one in the Italian sunshine.

All her good intentions about slowing things down with Luca, possibly stopping them altogether, had come to nothing. The present was too irresistible. Luca was too irresistible.

And where he was concerned she was proving all too weak.

Twenty pairs of eyes were looking at her expectantly, with interest. This wasn't the time to brood. She had a job to do—and it felt good. Minty took a breath and launched into her spiel. 'One of the tasks Luca has asked me to take on is raising awareness of Di Tore Dolce at home and in both new and existing markets. After all...' she smiled round at the attentive faces '...I have had some success at getting my name into the papers.'

As the board members chuckled approvingly, Minty began to relax and swung smoothly into the presentation she had been painstakingly preparing over the past few days. 'I wanted to really play to our strengths,' she explained, as picture after picture of the staff and local countryside flashed up on the screen. 'To me that's the absolute authenticity of our brand; the loyalty and love of our employees. Abroad that will play as bringing a taste of Italy into their lives; here, it's about localism, patriotism.'

It was working like a charm. The late nights, the trawling through market research, the time spent out and about talking to staff, filming and photographing them, was beginning to pay off. At times Minty had felt so far from her comfort zone, so out of her depth, that she had wanted to hand the whole project over to someone more experienced and return to scooping out *gelato* in the café. But each time she'd wavered Luca had been there, encouraging her, providing a sounding board, asking the right questions.

Believing in her.

As Minty went through the facts and figures, the research, the conclusions, her confidence began to rise. It was working. The board looked engaged, interested. Convinced.

'To keep costs low and to promote our image as a family-run, local business, we have decided against a glossy campaign. Instead we want to utilise social media, kick-started by some strategically placed adverts,' she said. 'These will lead people on to all our different social media platforms, where they can view recipes and short videos all presented by our best asset—our staff. As you can see from this sample I mocked up.'

As the video ran she anxiously scanned the faces of the board members to see their reaction. She had used Alfonso and Gianni, the delivery drivers she had travelled with just a few weeks before. Framed leaning against their cab, the rolling hills of Oschia lush and green behind them, they discussed their favourite ice-cream flavours, laughing and joking as they did so.

'I want our people to be the face of the company,' Minty continued as the closing credits rolled. 'From the people who make the *gelato* to those who deliver it; from the man who looks after the cows to the graphic designer. If they share why they are passionate about what we do, then they will hopefully inspire passion in our customers too.

'The plan is to make it interactive. People can discuss their favourite combinations online, post their recipes. Three or four times a year we'll run competitions and ask people to design their perfect flavour or combination and produce them as seasonal specials.'

She smiled around at the attentive board. It had gone well; she could tell. The atmosphere was optimistic, excited. 'Any questions?'

* * *

'You were brilliant in there.'

A sense of *déjà vu* shivered down Minty's spine; once again she was back in Luca's office, once again waiting for a meeting with the sales director. It was as if nothing had changed.

Yet everything had.

'I think you should accompany the sales team to some of the preliminary appointments, especially to the British ones,' Luca continued. 'They all speak the language, but there may be some subtle cultural nuances that they miss. The first appointment is in three weeks' time; will that work for you?'

'Should do,' Minty said, reaching for her iPad and pulling up her diary. 'I'm not sure what an asset I'll be, though. I have a certain reputation in the UK, remember?'

'I have every faith in you.' Luca shuffled some papers onto the table and began to point out some figures and projections. Minty barely heard him.

It was pleasantly warm in the office but a sudden chill shocked through her, goose-bumping her arms. Her heartbeat got louder and louder, the blood thrumming in her ears drowning out every sound. Was that really the date? In which case...

Numbly she began to count backwards. She must have made a mistake, surely? But, no; not last week, or the one before, or the one before that. In fact, not since before the trip to Sorrento.

She was nearly ten days late.

But I'm never late.

Minty shook her head in denial. It could be the stress of the move to Italy, the worry over Gio. She could have got her dates wrong.

Her stomach twisted, nausea rising, choking her. This couldn't be happening. Not now. Not when she was actually, finally, audaciously happy.

Why did she have to mess everything up? It was like she'd been made with a self-destruct button ready to detonate the second she got comfortable. 'I have to go home,' she broke in, interrupting Luca as he continued to discuss the trip overseas, unable to meet his eye, even to look at him. Her vision blurred. 'I'm sorry, but I don't feel well.'

Concern filled his voice. 'What's wrong, *cara*? You've gone so pale. I don't think you should be driving. Why don't you rest here and I'll get someone to drive you back?'

'No, thanks. I'll be fine.' Minty tried to muster up a smile, to allay his worry. The last thing she needed was company. She had to get to a chemist—not in the village, where anybody could see her, but in the next town along. Somewhere she could be anonymous. She had to know.

Oh, God, what if? She thrust the thought aside. This couldn't happen to her. It mustn't. They had been so careful.

Hadn't they?

Luca pressed redial yet again, trying to dampen down the worry that engulfed him each time Minty's phone went straight to voicemail. People didn't pick up for a variety of reasons. She could be in the bath or sleeping; she could have forgotten to recharge her phone. Just because a person wasn't available didn't mean they were lying in a crumpled car, dying.

She could have fainted and hit her head, though. She

had gone so pale so quickly; something was clearly wrong. He shouldn't have let her go home alone.

The all-too-familiar panic threatened his carefully built peace. It had taken years after the accident for him to be able to relax, not to be consumed by worry at a minute's tardiness. But Minty wasn't late, she was simply unavailable. Everything was fine. He was over-reacting.

Luca took a deep breath and tried to concentrate on the report in front of him but after ten minutes he pushed it to one side irritably. He hadn't taken in a word. He checked his phone again. Nothing. She had been gone for three hours.

He tapped his fingers on the desk. Sitting here worrying was achieving nothing. He should just work from home, keep an eye on her. And when he got back to find out she was absolutely fine, well, he would feel like a fool and know better next time.

His mind made up, he swept his papers into a file and snapped the laptop shut. He'd be home in ten minutes.

Thank God.

As Luca turned into the driveway, the first thing he noticed was the small Fiat parked haphazardly across the driveway. At least she was here, not in a ditch, over-turned in a field or wrapped around a tree.

Even by his standards, though, his panic had been over the top. After all, he *knew* that he overreacted—the grief therapy Rose had insisted he undergo had taught him that much self-awareness, after all. Did it mean his feelings went further than affection and attraction, further than the sense of responsibility he felt for her?

Luca was afraid of the answer. Afraid his feelings didn't just go further but also deeper.

Much deeper.

She had never promised anything more than a short time. She had never promised him anything at all.

He'd never asked her to. But what if he did? What if she agreed to stay? Not just tomorrow and for the rest of the summer but permanently?

For a moment Luca sat still, the car door half-open, paralysed by the sense that somehow his life would never be the same. Even if he said nothing, did nothing, he'd know. He'd know that maybe this was something more. What had she said—that he might find love somewhere unexpected?

The short walk to the house seemed to take an eternity, with Luca torn between a growing excitement at the thought of seeing Minty and finding out if he was right, that this was more than just a fling, and the same old dread. The dread that someone he cared about was ill, unconscious or worse.

This was the downside of letting someone in.

The possibility of losing them.

The door was unlocked. Luca opened it as quietly as he could and stepped carefully into the hall. If Minty was asleep, then he didn't want to wake her. It struck him how transformed the hallway was. Before, it had been neat, impersonal. The coat he used had hung tidily on the hat stand, a pair of polished shoes by the door. Now the hat stand was draped in an array of jackets, wraps and scarves like a rainbow Christmas tree. Shoes were piled up by the door in a heap of velvet and leather, his own providing a sturdy, dark contrast to the light, flimsy ballet shoes and flip-flops.

And hitting him the second he walked in was that elusive scent of lemons.

Luca stopped for a moment and inhaled, letting the fragrance wrap round him, breathing her in. He had been born in this house, raised in it, and now he owned it. It finally felt like home.

He stood at the bottom of the stairs listening out for a clue to Minty's whereabouts. Despite the shift in their relationship, she still had her own room—although she hadn't slept in there since their trip.

But the house was silent and empty. A quick search later, Luca admitted defeat. She was nowhere to be seen.

Luca paused at the open doorway to her room. The hallway was a haven of tidiness and order compared to here: clothes, shoes and bags lay tangled on the floor, the chairs and the pretty wooden bed Minty had used since she'd been a child. Powder was spilled on the cluttered chest of drawers and Luca could count at least three empty glasses and two cups. He smiled, remembering Rose's exasperation with Minty's untidiness. It was only ever in her personal space, though; in the office, in the living areas of the house, she was perfectly tidy.

Boarding-school training, she always said.

He turned around to check the spare bedrooms, unlikely as it was she would be in there, and stopped. He usually wouldn't invade her space but the glasses had been in there for several days now; she wouldn't mind if he collected them up and took them downstairs, would she?

After all, they were no longer warring teenagers with Keep Out signs plastered aggressively to their doors.

There was more crockery than Luca had been expecting and he ended up with a pile by the door bigger than he could safely carry. Deciding to return with a tray, he had one last quick scan round the room, making sure he hadn't missed anything, his eyes moving quickly past the heap of clothes on the bed before tracking back. Wasn't that the dress she had been wearing today? So whatever she was doing, wherever she was, she had come home and got changed.

Luca walked over to the bed and picked up the discarded outfit, a light shift-dress in a pretty sky-blue. It was definitely today's outfit; he recognised the white piping on the seams and the neckline. As he lifted it off the bed, he caught sight of a white leather bag underneath it, her phone and keys clearly visible through the open zip.

So that was why she hadn't picked up. And if her bag was here she must be close by. He'd put himself through all that for nothing. Again. *Let that be a lesson to you*, Luca told himself sternly, although his heart was racing with relief. He picked up the bag, meaning to put it on the floor so he could lay the dress flat, and froze. Inside, next to the keys, the purse, the phone and all the other paraphernalia she insisted on carrying around with her, was a white box. In black letters Luca saw just one word.

Gravidanza.

It was a pregnancy test.

And hope soared through him as true and sweet as a perfect summer's day.

'Luca?'

Minty stopped at the doorway. Had he seen it? What was he thinking?

Nausea twisted her stomach.

'What are you doing in here?'

Luca turned to her and her heart sank. He had the box in his hands.

But much worse was the look on his face. The hope.

She tried to speak, but her throat was so dry the words wouldn't come. Minty swallowed and tried again. 'I was just checking,' she said. 'I knew we'd been careful, but I was late. I'm never late. I got a bit panicky and bought three more tests than I needed.'

He was still looking so damned hopeful, so *expectant*. She grimaced at the unfortunate choice of words.

'I'd have come with you.'

She acknowledged his words with a faint nod. 'I know, but I didn't want to worry you, not if there wasn't a reason.'

'What did it say?' She knew he was trying to sound calm, but the excitement lit up his eyes; his body was held so still.

Minty closed her eyes briefly; it hurt to look at him. 'Don't worry,' she said. 'False alarm.' She could hear her voice, light and inconsequential, as if they were discussing the weather or what to have for dinner. Her eyes skittered to his and reluctantly registered the disappointment on his face. She quickly looked away and stared down at her hands twisting nervously.

Luca moved closer, the hope fading fast, replaced with concern. 'Are you okay?'

She laughed, the brittle sound foreign to her own ears. 'Of course, I was worried for a few minutes, naturally, but everything is okay. Nothing's changed. Only I'm a bit tired; I might have a bath.'

Only, of course, everything had changed—and he knew it too.

'Minty,' he said coaxingly. 'Let's go and have a glass of wine first. I want to talk to you.'

She considered refusing. The last thing she wanted was to talk to him about this, to disappoint him. She stood still for a second, still looking at him, then took a deep breath and nodded.

Neither of them spoke as they walked down the stairs and into the kitchen, Minty clutching the bag containing the traitorous box. Luca selected a bottle of Barolo and opened it, pouring out a glass for Minty and handing it to her. Their hands touched as she took the glass and she jumped, the contact shocking her. She took a large mouthful, barely registering the taste.

Luca took a sip of the wine, looking at her steadily. His voice was calm, steady. Completely sincere. 'This is real, you and me.'

Minty had heard many declarations of love but nothing this raw, this honest. His words burned themselves on her heart, a painful branding. He didn't need to say it. She knew.

She couldn't answer him. The tears were choking her throat, filling her eyes, sheer willpower alone keeping them from falling.

'Minty.' He gestured to her bag, at the box and all it implied. 'We could have this, share this, if you want to. I know we haven't been together long.' He laughed, an abrupt sound, loud in the quiet room. 'But in a way it feels like we've been heading here for ever.'

'No.' Just one quiet word. She moved forward slightly, her hands in front of her, as if she were warding him off. 'Don't say anything else, please.'

She couldn't bear it if he said anything else. Because he was right: they had been heading here all along and she had been too much of a coward to stop it.

'I want to,' Minty went on. Because she owed him that at least; she owed him the truth. She didn't give that to most people, she was rarely honest with herself, but it was all she had for him now. 'I can see it, you know. Working together, living here. And you; most of all I can see you, and I can see us. I can even imagine *this*.' She pulled the box out of the bag and threw it on the counter.

His head jerked up at that and she saw the hope, real and desperate. She had to crush it. 'It wouldn't last. I'm a player, Luca. I don't mean to be, but eventually you'll realise that I'm not real enough. They always do.'

'You don't know that.' Luca stepped forward and grasped her wrists, pulling her in close, the length of her body pulled next to him. She closed her eyes for a moment and breathed him in, allowed herself one last moment of safety, of contentment. 'We could try.'

Minty stepped back decisively, shaking her head. One day he would understand. When he was sat round the table with his wife and four children, and she was in yet another toxic break-up, he'd know that he was much, much better off without her.

This man had lost too much. He needed stability; he needed a family, love, someone who would put him first. And how she wanted to be that person; the need burned through her. But she couldn't risk it. 'It's too dangerous,' she said, begging him to understand, to see that she was doing this for him. That she loved him enough to be strong where he couldn't.

She'd always hoped that one day she could be a better person. She'd had no idea it would hurt so much.

'Dangerous how?'

Minty looked at him in surprise. 'Because of the children, of course.'

'Children?' he echoed.

'You want children, don't you?'

She could see the indecision on his face as he tried to work out how to answer her, but she knew. Of *course* he wanted children. Desperately. The look on his face as he'd looked at the darned test had told her everything she needed to know.

He wanted a family, the whole deal: children, in the plural; lots of them. One of those big family cars with sliding doors; a dog with a waving, feathery tail.

'Yes.' In the end he couldn't lie to her and she was grateful for that.

She smiled at him through the tears now free-falling down her face. 'When I'm with you, I want them too. You'll be a great dad—' Her voice broke and she swallowed convulsively. 'I'd rush into it, because that's what I do. We'd have a baby within a year.'

'And would that be so bad?'

Minty swallowed. Right now it sounded pretty close to perfect. But that was how things always were with her. 'Not at first. At first it would be amazing. But then I'd be tired; you'd be away, and I wouldn't mean to get bored and lonely, but I would. And the fantasy would fade.'

'You don't know that.'

She shook her head, trying to convince him, to make him see. 'Oh, I do. And as it faded you would get more and more disappointed in me.' Her voice quavered again. 'Because I wouldn't be the woman you wanted me to be, the person you thought I was. You see, I am very good at turning myself into the perfect partner, but I haven't learnt to sustain it yet.'

'I don't want you to sustain anything.' The sincerity in his voice nearly broke her. 'I just want you, the real you.'

But she had to stay strong. This wasn't for her, it was for him. 'I'd drift away, to Hollywood, or Spain or Argentina. Find a new person to be. I'd break your heart and that would be bad. But worse, much worse, I'd break my daughter's heart and I don't want to be that person. I can't be that person.'

'Minty!' With a muttered curse Luca stepped forward, his hands on her shoulders, swivelling her round to face him. 'You are not your mother!'

He was so wrong. 'I'm her daughter, in every way. And you deserve better, Luca.' She stepped forward and kissed him on the cheek, inhaling the scent of him one last time. 'I hope you find her,' she whispered in his ear. 'And she won't be a fantasy girl, she'll be real and loving and warm, and she will be a great mother.' She stepped back. 'You'll be so busy you'll forget all about me,' she said brightly. 'And that's the way it should be.'

'Don't do this again,' Luca said urgently. 'Don't run away.'

'It's what I do, Luca. I'm so, so sorry.'

Every fibre in her body was screaming at her to go to him, to change her mind, to try. But she wouldn't. He deserved better; he deserved more than she would ever be able to give him. He deserved somebody real who would be there no matter what.

If she'd loved him a little less, she might have stayed. Instead, she turned and she walked away.

CHAPTER ELEVEN

'How do I look? Like a junior account executive?' Minty twirled round, showing off the sharp lines of her black trouser suit. 'I quite like the collar, don't you? And the white piping is pretty sharp.'

'You look like you are going to a funeral, darling. Oh, Min, the interview sounds so dreary. PowerPoint presentations and pitches? *Eurgh.* Ditch it and come shopping with me instead. You know you want to. I'll treat you to a blow-dry and treatment, and then you can stop with those horrid chignons.'

Minty smiled at Fenella, who was stretched out like a cat on the extremely trendy and extremely uncomfortable sofa. 'I can't, Fen. I know it's a shock, but I actually need a job.'

'I don't see why,' Fenella grumbled. 'Your daddy will give in eventually, they always do. And you can stay here as long as you need. Besides, when your shares money comes in, you won't need to work, will you?'

'It's not enough to sustain me in privileged idleness for ever, and you know I'm planning to invest in a flat.' A sharp pain stabbed through her at the thought of the shares. The sooner they were sold back to Luca, the better, then all ties would be cut. Finally, this time.

'Ooh, you could be in luck. I heard from Mrs Harrison that there may be an opening here.' Fenella brightened up. 'Not as lovely as my penthouse but a very reasonable corner apartment, so nice and light. We could go and have a look this afternoon.'

'Chelsea is a little out of my league now,' Minty said, repressing a sigh. She wasn't asking for more than market value for her shares and, thanks to Luca's policy of reinvesting most of the profits straight back into the business, she doubted she would get enough to buy a shoebox in central London. 'I'll be lucky to manage Zone Two; I may even have to venture south of the river.'

'Don't be so barbaric, darling. And you can't possibly live in a building without a concierge and a gym! Oh, Minty, it all sounds so grim. Forget the job; there must be another way. I know, I'll talk to Hugo. He always said he'd love to have you at the gallery because you actually know something about art. Think of all the lovely, rich men you'll meet, and you can stay here as long as you want. It'll be fun.'

Fun and really tempting: sinking back into her old carefree ways; pretending Italy had never happened, pretending Luca had never happened. After all, she had done it before.

Only, last time she had slipped away in the night, hadn't had to face the consequences of her actions. But it had been better to hurt him now than later on. Better to hurt him now than allow him the time to become disillusioned with her. The shock and pain in his eyes had wounded her; facing his inevitable disappointment and rejection would have been a fatal blow. She should have got out sooner.

She should never have started at all. But no more. She was a new Minty. If she didn't learn from this, if the constant pain didn't remind her, then she wasn't worth saving.

'That's really sweet, but I think I have to do this on my own. I do really appreciate everything you are doing, but it's not just about the money. I actually enjoyed working,' Minty said, smiling at the shock on Fenella's face. 'And I do really want this job. So, tell me, do I look like a sober, responsible, hard-working young lady?'

Fenella looked her up and down then shook her head in disgust. 'Why are women's suits so ugly?' she complained. 'But, if boring and neat is the look you are going for, then you have achieved it.'

'Thank you, I think.'

'So this is it?' Fenella said. 'Nine to five, a small flat somewhere on the end of a Tube line, suits and flat boots? Too tired to come out on a weeknight, and homemade lasagne and bring-your-own on a Saturday? I don't know what happened in Italy, Minty, but you need to get over it. Punishing yourself helps nobody.'

'This is how most people live, Fen.' But the vision that Fenella's words conjured up was depressing: long days, long commutes back to a small flat for a ready meal for one and the latest reality show on TV. Minty tried desperately to remember the positives: the creativity of work, being self-sufficient, being herself.

Whoever that may be.

It's time to find out, she told herself grimly. Before she blundered into anyone else's life, hurt anyone else. Before she hurt herself even more than she had done. Each time it got harder and harder to pick herself up.

There had been moments during the past few weeks when she had thought she wouldn't be able to carry on. That falling into the mire of lethargy and depression and allowing herself to sink was the only thing she could do.

And yet here she was, still standing—just.

Fenella was shaking her head. 'But, Minty, you're not most people. Of all your projects, this is definitely the dreariest, I give it two months before you're bored, tops. Just make sure you don't burn all your bridges before then, okay?'

'This is different. Honest, Fen, I know what I'm doing. A brand-new, man-free start far under the tabloids' radar is exactly what the doctor ordered. Right, I'm off. Wish me luck?'

But as Minty exited the apartment Fenella's words echoed in her ears. She desperately wanted to change, to anchor herself down with the responsibilities of work and routine, but what if she couldn't? What if she threw it all up for the illusion of love again?

Except she wouldn't. For her heart was back in Italy, with Luca. And Minty wasn't sure she'd ever be able to retrieve it. She was done with illusions.

If only reality wasn't so bleak. And so very, very lonely.

'I think we should resurrect the summer party.'

Luca looked up in surprise. Although Gio had been working in his office for the past couple of hours, he had been so quiet Luca had almost forgotten he was there. 'Summer party?' he echoed.

'It was your father's favourite event of the year,' Gio said, leaning back in his chair and stretching, a reminiscent smile on his lips. 'We would have a conference in the morning for all staff, a way of updating them on what the plans were for the year ahead. Of course, there were a lot fewer in those days. Di Tore Dolce wasn't quite the empire you have made it.' He looked fondly over at his nephew.

'I remember,' Luca said slowly, dredging up memories of carousels, ice cream and the annual 'factory versus managers' football match—usually a good-tempered affair. 'There would be a huge barbeque in the evening and we would invite all the employees' families. There were fireworks.'

'We cancelled it the year your parents died,' Gio said. 'Somehow the time never felt right to reinstate it. But this year, with the expansion, the new marketing plan to unveil, the ads…the time is right, I think. Don't you agree?'

Luca didn't answer at first. He didn't feel remotely like a party, even a company one. All he wanted to do was work, work until he was so tired he could fall into bed and into a dreamless, exhausted sleep. Work until there was no room for thoughts, for memories, for regrets.

But Gio had obviously not received the 'no fun' memo. He was full of ideas. 'I thought we could introduce an awards ceremony as a thank-you for all the hard work people have been putting in, only without prizes but with personalised *gelato*. It all fits in with the new campaign, and it's a really personal thank-you, too.'

'*Si*, it's a good idea.' It was. And it was great to see Gio involved and enthused. If only Luca could feel it too. If only he could feel anything.

'I also think you should invite Minty.' Gio sounded so placid, as if he was discussing whether to hold the ceremony indoors or in a marquee; whether to have a carousel or a Ferris wheel. But of course Luca had told him so little. Just that Minty had, true to form, got bored with corporate life and rural living and had headed back to London. That she was cutting her ties once and for all, surrendering her shares.

As Luca had foreseen. As he had wanted.

If only she'd done it earlier.

But of course Gio must know there was more to it. He had spent time with them, had come to dinner, on days out. They had been discreet but not that discreet; it had been impossible for Luca not to touch her.

His stomach clenched, his fingers suddenly impossibly cold. Empty. They ached to feel that warm, smooth flesh just one more time.

A sharp pain was a welcome distraction as his nails bit into his palm, wrestling for control with his treacherous body. There was no point in missing her. She was never coming back.

'I know it was a shock when Rose left her share of the company to Minty,' Gio said. Luca could feel his sharp eyes on him and forced himself to appear calm, uninterested in the conversation.

'They were her shares,' he said lightly, focussing on the screen in front of him, although he couldn't make out a single word.

'She thought you had a tremendous future, you know,' Gio continued. 'That's why she backed your plans. And thank goodness she did. Look how unreliable the banks have been the past few years. I know you're sharp, Luca, and if anyone can be successful in these dreadful times it's you, but it's been a blessing not to be burdened with bank loans.'

'I have always been very grateful to Rose for everything, not just investing in the company.' It was an understatement. Not only had she given up her life in London to raise him but she'd handed over her inheritance to a nineteen-year-old boy with big plans and bigger dreams. If only she'd lived to see the fruition of those dreams.

'But Minty was her niece. Rose wanted to make sure she was included, would still be part of the family when she was gone. That's why she left half of her part of the business to her. To keep her close, give her those ties. Don't let her go without a fight, Luca. Make her see that she belongs here, that she is part of us.'

Don't you think I've tried?

But had he? Had he fought or had he just let her walk away, talk herself out of their future, out of his life?

When he tried to remember that evening, there was just a blurred tangle of feelings. The worry at her absence, the surprise at the realisation that she meant so much more to him than he had ever imagined, the shocking hope when he'd seen the test. And then the crushing of his dreams as she'd rejected him, rejected a future with him, had walked away.

But what he couldn't remember was what he'd said. If he had said enough, or if he had bowed to the inevitability of her departure.

And if he hadn't fought for her, well, then, he was no better than the three starter-fiancés. He was worse.

No, he had tried. Hadn't he?

'She doesn't want to be here, Gio.'

'Doesn't she? She looked pretty happy to me.'

She had been happy. Until the end. Until she'd seen a future trapped with him.

'At first.' Luca shrugged. 'But you know Minty. Always fluttering off to the next thing.'

Gio looked at him, his eyes shrewd, knowing. Uncomfortable. 'Minty reminds me of Rose in many ways, and your mother, a little: city girls on the outside, but at heart? They belong here. In Oschia. None of them meant to settle here, but they did. Their souls belonged here.'

That was what Luca had wanted to believe, had hoped.

He shook his head. 'It's too late, Gio. She's gone.'

'Then it's up to you to bring her back, to convince her to stay. I'll get her to come to the party but the rest is up to you. If you love her, Luca, you'll find a way.'

If he loved her? Of course he loved her.

Minty. Lady Araminta Henrietta Davenport. For goodness' sake, what kind of name was that? And yet, it suited her. It was fresh, quirky, unique.

If she'd been an ice cream, she'd have been more than the obvious, a *gelato* miles away from the usual *menta* flecked with chocolate chips. A delicate sorbet—mint mixed with elderflower, maybe—or perhaps something richer, more decadent? Dark chocolate, of course; maybe something alcoholic. Lime juice and a touch of rum mixed with mint, her namesake? Or how about something quirky and sweet: peppermint swirled with chocolate bunnies?

Luca's mind was racing. How would he define Minty? Vibrant yet vulnerable. Sophisticated and sweet. Proud and passionate. Impulsive and intoxicating.

He pulled a piece of paper towards him and began to sketch out a series of ingredients and combinations, images flashing through his mind as he did so: Minty walking through the countryside, listening, comforting. Minty perched on his desk, flushed with the success of her work, hair back, tired after a long shift away. Minty wrapped round him, long limbs and smooth skin, utterly desirable.

How could he have let her walk away?

If he wasn't so scared of losing everyone he loved

then maybe he would have thought to fight. He hadn't fought for Gio; he'd needed Minty to push him. Now Gio was repaying the favour. But Luca shouldn't have needed that push. He should have made her see, made her stay. Let her know he wasn't going down without a fight.

The old fear was nothing compared to this. Luca knew all too well how much it hurt to lose the ones you loved, but never loving them at all? Infinitely worse.

The inertia of the past few weeks was gone. Energy and excitement flooded through him. She thought he didn't understand her; that he was in love with a phantom, a cipher?

It was time to show Lady Araminta that she didn't know as much as she thought she did.

It was time to take control. And this time her knight in shining armour was determined not just to win the battle; he was going to win the whole damned war.

CHAPTER TWELVE

IT WAS ODD to be back.

It was just a few weeks since Minty had packed up her bags to get the first budget flight back to the UK, yet in some ways it seemed a lifetime ago. Ensconced in Fenella's luxurious Chelsea pad—invites to parties, launches and society events pinging into her inbox; the same crowd, the same haunts, the same gossip—it was as if she had never been gone. Each day Italy retreated further and further away.

Night-times, however, were a different matter. She woke up still feeling the warmth of the sun, smelling the ripening olive trees, hearing Luca call her name. She woke up running her hands over the ripple of muscle under smooth, tanned skin, feeling the caress of his skilled, knowing hands, the touch of his lips.

Minty shivered.

Coming back would help. It had to help. She needed to convince her treacherous, yearning heart that this was just a place, that he was just a man and that she could move on. She would sell him her shares and then she could find a nice little flat in a sensible part of town and start the new job she had worked so hard to get. She would be sober and respectable and achieve something by herself, for herself.

It was a laudable aim.

If she thought too much about the lonely reality of the life she faced, she would cry.

But not here. She was here because Gio had made it clear it would mean a lot to him if she showed up, would mean a lot to the employees who were so excited about launching the new campaign, the campaign she was responsible for.

And because had Luca insisted she sell him her shares in person. Obviously, she had intended to tell him to stuff his money and stuff his shares. Unfortunately a quick glance at the London rental market had persuaded her that discretion was very much the best part of valour. It turned out that junior account executives did not earn enough to rent their own flats, or even to share a flat anywhere Minty had heard of. It would be much easier to start her new, self-sufficient life if she wasn't sharing a house with five other people a two-hour commute away from work.

Besides, this time she had to say goodbye, make sure the door was firmly shut. Otherwise she would never move on. For his sake, she had to.

He deserved better.

And maybe one day she would deserve something good too.

Okay, enough introspection. Any more maudlin thoughts and she'd be back to writing 'nobody understands me' poetry, and that behaviour was not acceptable in anyone over the age of fifteen. She would go in, she would smile and she would make polite conversation.

Then she would collect her cheque and leave.

The summer conference was being held in the large field that lay next to the office. Usually full of peacefully grazing cows, it had been cleared and cleaned for the day's festivities. A large marquee erected at the far end was ready for the business part of the day; the remainder of the field was filled with carnival rides and food stalls, all complimentary—even the large beer tent. Mid-afternoon, the workers' families would arrive and the party half of the event would begin. Minty was planning to be long gone by that point.

She looked over at the marquee and her stomach lurched in panic. What did people know about her departure? To walk in, an object of curiosity to every person there, to find a seat and make polite conversation—she suddenly feared it was beyond her. She might have graced the cover of every tabloid, every gossip rag, in the UK but that wasn't really her. That was just a persona, a created image. She didn't give a toss what the readers of those papers thought. 'Tomorrow's fish-and-chip wrappings,' her grandmother said.

Of course, nobody wrapped their fish and chips in newspaper any more, but Minty appreciated the sentiment.

Yet somehow, improbably, she cared far too much about what the three hundred employees of Di Tore Dolce thought. She didn't want them to feel let down, to hold her in contempt.

She cared far too much about what Luca thought.

Minty shifted her weight from foot to foot nervously, the temptation to turn back almost overwhelming her. After all, nobody knew she was actually here.

'Minty, *bella.* You're a sight for sore eyes. Have you lost weight? You need to eat more.' Gio materialised behind her, gathering her to him in a warm hug.

Minty clung on to Gio gratefully. 'My flatmate only eats canapés; it's quite the diet.'

'Barbaric English. We need to feed you up. The meeting's about to start but let's see what we can find.' And, tucking her hand through his arm, Gio led her off towards the big tent, keeping up a flow of voluble conversation that required Minty to do little but nod agreement or add the odd 'mmm'.

In less than a couple of minutes they were at the large tent and Gio was ushering her inside. The tent was nearly full of laughing, chattering employees, sitting in long rows, facing a wide stage that ran along the width of the tent. A row of chairs on the stage looked out towards the audience and Gio steered Minty in their direction after snagging her a large cup of coffee and a plate filled with cheese, fruit and little pastries.

'Oh, no,' she said in some alarm at the thought of facing so many pairs of eyes. 'Gio, this isn't right. I'm not going to be on the board for much longer. I was planning a discreet seat at the back. Besides, I can't eat this lot with everyone staring at me.'

'We're launching your campaign today, it's only right you take a seat on the stage,' Gio admonished her, but he stopped and gave the plate in her hand an assessing glance. 'But there's still five minutes before we need to be seated. If you stand here in this corner, nobody will see you. I'll be back for you soon.' He directed her to a discreet corner of the tent behind the lectern and the large screen that dominated the stage, pulling up a spare chair and telling her to 'Eat up, there's a good girl.' It was like being a child accompanying him to work again. Minty found it strangely comforting, allowing someone else to make the decisions.

Leaning back against the rough canvas of the tent, Minty looked at the plate. Nausea twisted her stomach. She couldn't eat a thing despite the early start and the lack of breakfast. She just wanted to get the meeting with Luca over with and to leave. She placed the plate on the chair gingerly and clasped the coffee cup closer, dropping her head to inhale the rich aroma.

'Are you going to drink that or snort it?'

Luca.

An unexpected, fierce joy filled her. She lifted her head and looked at him, aiming for friendly and causal. 'Hello.' To her annoyance, her voice came out breathy and she swallowed desperately, trying to get some moisture back into her dry mouth. 'You look well.'

He did. Disgustingly well. He obviously wasn't missing her at all.

Yet seeing him was like coming home. What was she doing, battling to forge a new, different life in London? She'd had a new life here and thrown it all away simply because she'd been scared.

And it was too late. Luca was looking at her quizzically, possibly even affectionately, but he didn't seem at all bothered by her presence. 'You look tired.'

Well, that did a lot for a girl's confidence. 'You know how we party girls are with our late nights and early-morning flights.'

He nodded unsmilingly. 'We're about to start. Do you want any of that?'

Minty looked at the plate of food and shook her head. 'Gio insisted, but I'm not really hungry.'

'Okay, then, shall we?' He took her arm, and at just that light touch a tingle ran up Minty's arm, snaking down her spine. Her treacherous knees weakened in response. *Pull yourself together*, she told herself sharply, pulling her elbow out of his grasp.

'I can manage, thanks.'

Luca threw her an amused glance but didn't comment, instead leading the way across the tangle of wires at the back of the stage, standing aside to allow her to mount the stairs before him.

Standing up there, alone, three hundred pairs of eyes fastened on her, was terrifying. Minty resisted the temptation to wipe her palms on her skirt; resisted the even bigger temptation to scuttle away as fast as her suddenly tight, crushing heels would allow. Instead she allowed herself to meet the eyes, searching out familiar faces: Gianni, Alfonso, Natalia. She braced herself to see contempt, dislike, disgust; instead, the frank, welcoming smiles that greeted her almost overwhelmed her. She held each of the gazes, answering the smiles with one of her own, blinking back the tears that had sprung unexpectedly to her eyes.

Was she planning to throw all of this away? Leave the sweet-smelling countryside for the London fog? Leave the fresh air for two hours a day jostled against someone's armpit on the Tube? Leave a company where she was respected and loved for a junior position in a place where she knew no one?

Was she planning to leave Luca?

Only it didn't seem as if he cared one way or another. Maybe she could stay here anyway. She had done a good job, even he accepted that. She could just stay out of his way, watch as he found someone stable and steady, moved on.

Just the thought of it was like a punch to the stomach. She couldn't do that—and that was why she'd have to say goodbye.

'Buongiorno.' Without even a glance at her, Luca strode to the lectern and began proceedings. For all the formal business—board reports, sales figures, expansion plans—it was a lively presentation. Luca was un-

expectedly funny and charming in parts, serious and focussed in others. It was mesmerising. The whole room was quiet, all their attention on the tall man who obviously loved his work, their work, so passionately.

Minty shivered. Suddenly all she wanted was his attention; for some of that passion to be directed at her; to see heat in those golden eyes. Even anger would be better than amusement. Emotion would show he cared.

Not that she deserved it, but surely if there was love there was forgiveness? That was the fairy tale anyway. Rose had forgiven her time after time, had been there no matter what. She was the only person who had been. Could Luca live up to her legacy?

Was she even worth it?

Minty was jolted out of her thoughts as the lights dimmed and the familiar music filled the room, the tune that accompanied the videos posted to the web. She had seen a couple of them many times, obsessively editing to make them perfect in every way, whilst preserving the genuine naturalness that made them authentic. The others were new and watching the staff talk about why they loved their jobs—and, of course, their favourite *gelato* combination—was so moving that a lump formed in her throat and tears once again threatened, prickling the back of her eyes.

'Part of the campaign will include competitions for the public to win the chance for their ice-cream ideas to be made up into special editions,' Luca said as the lights came up. 'We thought we would kick-start that process with special editions designed around some of you, as a thank-you for some exceptional work this year. I would like to start off with Giulia. Would you like to come up here please?'

There were three winners overall. Luca congratulated each of them before presenting them with a glass of 'their' *gelato*, designed with their personalities in mind: sweet praline for the blushing, shy Giulia—a bold dark-chocolate and espresso for the taciturn Bruno; a sophisticated fruit and sorbet concoction for the elegant Marietta. Minty found herself applauding warmly as the three returned to their seats, aware that this signalled the end of the presentation. She had to face Luca again, sign whatever she needed to sign and leave. In an hour's time, this would all be behind her.

Luca's voice rang out, strong, confident. 'Okay, I have one more special award to give out to the woman who came up with the idea in the first place. Minty, would you like to come and receive your prize?'

Minty sat frozen in her chair. Surely he didn't mean her? Surely he wasn't turning to look at her, heat finally blazing out of his eyes? It was as if time had stopped, Luca's words echoing round and round in Minty's head. She blinked at him in disbelief.

'You made *me* an ice cream?' Her words were low, forced out of her by her shocked surprise, but he heard her, smiling across the stage at her with infinite tenderness.

'Of course. And it was harder than I expected. You know,' he said confidingly to the audience, 'this should have been the easiest of the lot, with a name like Minty! And yes, of course, mint was the starting flavour. But with what? Choc-chip? Too obvious, and our Minty is anything but. Eventually I decided that a light fruit base was required. I did try elderflower but, no, that wasn't quite right. Raspberry was too overpowering, *limon* too bitter. And then it hit me...' He paused dramatically and the audience waited expectantly.

Minty couldn't have moved if she'd wanted to. What

did Luca think encapsulated her? Marshmallow—sweet and insubstantial? Despite her love of lemon sorbet, she was glad he'd rejected it. She didn't want him to think her acidic and sour.

She shook herself. It was ice cream, just ice cream. And yet it felt like so much more. Anxiety gnawed away at her stomach. She couldn't stay silent, keep her cool any longer. 'So, what did you choose?'

Tawny eyes held hers, their expression completely serious, penetrating. 'A rich strawberry sorbet was the next step, but it was still missing something. I added dark chocolate and a hint of lime and it worked. It was delicious, but not yet complete. And then it hit me.' A smile entered the eyes still looking directly into hers until she felt dizzy, lost in the amber depths. 'It needed something light, fizzy but with unexpected depths... Prosecco.'

'Sounds delicious.' She couldn't say anything but platitudes but she was filled with a tumultuous mixture: gratitude; joy; longing. Longing for this man who stood opposite showing the world that he understood her. All of her. Many people thought they could sum up Lady Araminta Davenport in just a few words; thought they could pigeonhole her: rich, flighty, frivolous. And she was; she was all of those things. But she hoped, she knew, that she did have unexpected depths—only no one had ever wanted to dig deep enough to find out.

'Here.' He was holding a cone out to her. 'A cone, not a cup. A sugar cone, too.'

He'd remembered.

'It's the only way,' she said, getting to her feet, hoping she would make it across the stage to him. Slowly she walked across, her eyes fixed on his, and took it, holding the cone gingerly, almost afraid to try the sorbet. She took a hesitant nibble. Flavours flooded her mouth. The sweet richness of strawberry and swirls of dark chocolate were a sharp contrast to the freshness of mint set off by the hint of lime, the Prosecco a mild counterpart.

'What do you think?' Luca's assurance seemed to have deserted him; he was gazing at her anxiously.

'Perfect.' She couldn't think of anything else to say. 'Thank you, it's the nicest thing anyone has ever done for me.' Trite, yet truer than she could express.

The marquee erupted into applause as Gio came forward to congratulate her and round off the official part of the day. Minty stood caught in the spotlights for a moment, unsure where to go, relieved when Luca took her wrist and ushered her to the back of the stage and down the steps away from the glare of the lights, the noise and the attention.

She stood for a moment just staring at him, her eyes drinking in the rightness of him. The staff, the marquee and the occasion were disappearing. All that mattered was the tall man in a well-cut suit, dark hair falling over his forehead, a man with killer cheekbones and an even deadlier smile. He stood looking back at her, the smile replaced with something darker, hungrier, more intense.

'Thank you,' she said, concentrating on choosing the right words, on not letting his presence overwhelm her. 'For this.' She gestured with her ice cream. 'I can't tell you…' She stopped, caught her breath and couldn't continue, momentarily overwhelmed. She gave up and concentrated on the sorbet instead, as if there was nothing else, as if the man beside her was a mirage.

'Minty, look at me.' His voice was gentle, coaxing. Despite herself, she allowed him to take her chin and tilt her head up to meet his fiery gaze. 'I'm sorry I let you go.'

He was apologising to her? She shook her head. 'I was the one who left.'

Again. The unspoken word hung in the air.

'*Si*, you did.' Now it was Luca's turn to shrug ruefully, his hand moving from her chin to her shoulder, a light, tingling touch. 'But I let you go. I didn't fight for you. You needed someone to, and I didn't.'

Minty wanted to deny it but his words had a core of truth that pierced her. That was what she had been waiting for. Someone to fight for her, someone to rescue the little girl abandoned in an empty school; someone to show her that she was worth it, no matter what.

'I acted just like all those other fools,' Luca continued, his hand continuing to stroke her shoulder, his thumb tracing circles on the delicate skin at her neck. Minty wanted to lean into his caress like a cat, rub against the tantalisingly light touch. 'I allowed you to push me away. And by the time I came to my senses it was too late; you were gone. I nearly came to London—even the tiny matter of having no idea where you were didn't stop me booking a ticket, driving halfway to the airport. But I knew that I needed more than simply to turn up at your door, roses in hand and a prepared speech on my lips.'

What would she have done if he'd turned up at her door? Would she have shut him out? She was half-afraid she would have; half-sure she would have fallen on him and never, ever have let him go.

'Minty, I am a simple man, an ice-cream maker…'

'You're more than that!' she said impulsively. Was that really how this extraordinary man saw himself? 'You're so much more: a businessman, an employer, a farmer, a gentleman, a good friend and nephew... A lover.' The heat filled her cheeks as the memories of just how good a lover he was flooded through her, memories evoked by the torturous, languid caress.

He laughed softly, a warm, intimate sound. '*Grazie, cara*, but at heart an ice-cream maker. I thought, I hoped, if I could make you the perfect ice cream, somehow I could convince you that I know when you're playing a role. And that it wasn't businesswoman Minty or black-tie Minty or even Sorrento Minty I was falling for, although you are all of those people. It was the spoilt and wilful, serious and empathic, intelligent and resourceful, untrusting yet hopeful, loving you.'

Minty's hand had crept up to find Luca's. She linked her fingers through his, squeezing it convulsively. 'What if I hadn't shown up?' she whispered through the large lump forming in her throat.

Luca removed the hand from her shoulder, the fingers of his other hand tightening on hers reassuringly, promising that he would never let her go. 'I have a ticket,' he said, pulling out an airline ticket from his back pocket. 'The plane leaves tonight. There's a tub of 'Araminta' at the warehouse in London. I was pretty sure I could get it to you before it melted to slush.'

'The second I got here I wanted to stay. I knew I had made a mistake,' Minty said, looking up at him, reassured by the understanding and hot need in his eyes. 'In London I got by with pretending, throwing myself into getting a job—a real job—and preparing for a sensible future. But the nights were different. Every morning I had to start again.'

'You have a new job?'

Pride welled up inside her. 'I do, and without using my connections or my name to get it. I used my second name so that they took me seriously. I even had a real CV showcasing my time here and the work I did promoting the cupcake shops. It worked. You'd have been proud, I think. I'm meant to be starting next week, but...' Minty's voice trailed off. She wanted him to ask her to stay, tell her that he needed her, that the company needed her.

Only hadn't he already put himself on the line? He had made her an ice cream, bought tickets and planned a declaration. She had just shown up. It was time for her to face rejection. 'I haven't actually signed a contract. I mean, if you wanted me to stay...'

Minty wasn't sure of the response she wanted. Tears? To be gathered up in a hug? Hard, hot kisses right here and now, and sod the very real chance of discovery? Actually, she knew full well which response she wanted. Five minutes standing this close to Luca and barely touching him had her burning with the need to sink into him.

What she hadn't expected was for him to take a step back, to drop her hand and look at her intently. 'That's great, because I have something I want to ask you.'

Oh, no, those horribly familiar words. Possibly the phrase she hated most in the whole of the English language, even when they were said in an Italian accent. She hoped he wasn't going to get down on one knee.

She hoped she didn't say yes, even though part of her wanted to say yes more than anything else in the world.

Only his knee didn't even bend a little.

'I want you to take charge of all the overseas operations. I know you're inexperienced but I have a good team who will support you—and I think you've earned it.'

The words hammered themselves into Minty's

stunned brain. He wanted to offer her a job? He didn't want her body, her connections, her money—he wanted her brain. She stood still. 'This is all about work? Not about us?'

Where had those words come from? She should be happy, elated, that he recognised her hard work and saw her potential. That he was offering her such an important role. But she expected more, wanted more. Much more.

Although, he hadn't actually said that he loved her, had he? Just that he knew her and had fallen for her. Had she misinterpreted his meaning?

All doubt was banished as Luca pulled her tenderly in and dropped a kiss on the top of her head. Such a small, gentle kiss, yet it fizzed through her body like a firework, carrying hope and desire with it. 'Of course, I'm hoping that eventually you will move back in with me.'

Tears filled Minty's eyes. She couldn't look at him; all her attention was on the weave of his jacket at the shoulder, at the small vee of exposed throat, so close, so eminently kissable as he continued.

'I know I need to convince you that I love you, all of you—not the parts of you that fit my life but every part of you, all the untidy, ridiculous, shoe-wearing, variety-loving, city-girl bits that make you, Minty. I need to let you prove to yourself that I offered you this job because I would be crazy not to, not because I want you back with me. I'm hoping it doesn't take too long, because I miss you. Being near you and not being able to kiss you properly is driving me crazy, and I think that will only get worse. But I will wait, for as long as it takes. And when I do convince you...' Minty looked shyly up at him. 'I will not waste a single moment with an

engagement. I have no intention of being fiancé number four—I do, however, plan to be your one and only
husband.'

His tone was light, almost jocular, but the look in
his eyes told a different story. It was blazing sincerity
and need, love and desire. Minty stared back, tongue-
tied, unable to find the words. This was the boy who
had spent a day letting her win at games to make her
smile; the youth who'd taken her on a wild ride to make
her forget; the man who'd treated her like a grown-up.
This man was her first crush, her last lover.

Only Luca would spend days perfecting a recipe just
for her. No wonder she'd been so miserable; for the
first time, she'd found the man she didn't want to get
engaged to.

Instead she'd found the one man she wanted to spend
her whole life with.

'I get bored easily,' she felt she had to warn him. 'I
have more issues than the entire cast of a soap opera.
I'm irrational and selfish…'

The grip on her chin tightened. 'You're big-hearted
and whole-hearted and warm-hearted. You're you, and
that's all I need.'

Minty stared at him, this tall, sensual man with the
blazing eyes. How could she ever have thought him
stuffy or bossy? 'I need you too—' Her voice broke.
She had never said those words to anyone, had never
admitted needing anyone, not even to herself. 'I need
you and I love you and I want you, and I never want to
spend another day away from you.'

'You'll come home with me?'

Tears were running freely down Minty's face as she
rose onto her tiptoes and pressed her mouth against his,
luxuriating in the familiarity, the safety, the essence

of him. 'Of course I will,' she whispered against his mouth. 'I'll go anywhere with you. Anywhere.'

He stood back, just a little, and looked at her with infinite tenderness. 'We'll work it all out, Minty—marriage, children, we'll work it out together. As a team. And no matter what the future brings I'll be there, every step of the way.'

'I can face the future if I'm with you,' Minty told him and she meant it. She wasn't afraid any more. Wild excitement filled her, mingling with the happiness and desire. She was about to spend the rest of her life with this man, her biggest adventure yet.

And Minty couldn't wait.

* * * * *

Mills & Boon® Hardback

June 2014

ROMANCE

Ravelli's Defiant Bride	Lynne Graham
When Da Silva Breaks the Rules	Abby Green
The Heartbreaker Prince	Kim Lawrence
The Man She Can't Forget	Maggie Cox
A Question of Honour	Kate Walker
What the Greek Can't Resist	Maya Blake
An Heir to Bind Them	Dani Collins
Playboy's Lesson	Melanie Milburne
Don't Tell the Wedding Planner	Aimee Carson
The Best Man for the Job	Lucy King
Falling for Her Rival	Jackie Braun
More than a Fling?	Joss Wood
Becoming the Prince's Wife	Rebecca Winters
Nine Months to Change His Life	Marion Lennox
Taming Her Italian Boss	Fiona Harper
Summer with the Millionaire	Jessica Gilmore
Back in Her Husband's Arms	Susanne Hampton
Wedding at Sunday Creek	Leah Martyn

MEDICAL

200 Harley Street: The Soldier Prince	Kate Hardy
200 Harley Street: The Enigmatic Surgeon	Annie Claydon
A Father for Her Baby	Sue MacKay
The Midwife's Son	Sue MacKay

0514GEN STD HB

Mills & Boon® Large Print

June 2014

ROMANCE

A Bargain with the Enemy	Carole Mortimer
A Secret Until Now	Kim Lawrence
Shamed in the Sands	Sharon Kendrick
Seduction Never Lies	Sara Craven
When Falcone's World Stops Turning	Abby Green
Securing the Greek's Legacy	Julia James
An Exquisite Challenge	Jennifer Hayward
Trouble on Her Doorstep	Nina Harrington
Heiress on the Run	Sophie Pembroke
The Summer They Never Forgot	Kandy Shepherd
Daring to Trust the Boss	Susan Meier

HISTORICAL

Portrait of a Scandal	Annie Burrows
Drawn to Lord Ravenscar	Anne Herries
Lady Beneath the Veil	Sarah Mallory
To Tempt a Viking	Michelle Willingham
Mistress Masquerade	Juliet Landon

MEDICAL

From Venice with Love	Alison Roberts
Christmas with Her Ex	Fiona McArthur
After the Christmas Party...	Janice Lynn
Her Mistletoe Wish	Lucy Clark
Date with a Surgeon Prince	Meredith Webber
Once Upon a Christmas Night...	Annie Claydon

Mills & Boon® Hardback
July 2014

ROMANCE

Christakis's Rebellious Wife	Lynne Graham
At No Man's Command	Melanie Milburne
Carrying the Sheikh's Heir	Lynn Raye Harris
Bound by the Italian's Contract	Janette Kenny
Dante's Unexpected Legacy	Catherine George
A Deal with Demakis	Tara Pammi
The Ultimate Playboy	Maya Blake
Socialite's Gamble	Michelle Conder
Her Hottest Summer Yet	Ally Blake
Who's Afraid of the Big Bad Boss?	Nina Harrington
If Only...	Tanya Wright
Only the Brave Try Ballet	Stefanie London
Her Irresistible Protector	Michelle Douglas
The Maverick Millionaire	Alison Roberts
The Return of the Rebel	Jennifer Faye
The Tycoon and the Wedding Planner	Kandy Shepherd
The Accidental Daddy	Meredith Webber
Pregnant with the Soldier's Son	Amy Ruttan

MEDICAL

200 Harley Street: The Shameless Maverick	Louisa George
200 Harley Street: The Tortured Hero	Amy Andrews
A Home for the Hot-Shot Doc	Dianne Drake
A Doctor's Confession	Dianne Drake

0614GEN STD HB

Mills & Boon® Large Print
July 2014

ROMANCE

A Prize Beyond Jewels — Carole Mortimer
A Queen for the Taking? — Kate Hewitt
Pretender to the Throne — Maisey Yates
An Exception to His Rule — Lindsay Armstrong
The Sheikh's Last Seduction — Jennie Lucas
Enthralled by Moretti — Cathy Williams
The Woman Sent to Tame Him — Victoria Parker
The Plus-One Agreement — Charlotte Phillips
Awakened By His Touch — Nikki Logan
Road Trip with the Eligible Bachelor — Michelle Douglas
Safe in the Tycoon's Arms — Jennifer Faye

HISTORICAL

The Fall of a Saint — Christine Merrill
At the Highwayman's Pleasure — Sarah Mallory
Mishap Marriage — Helen Dickson
Secrets at Court — Blythe Gifford
The Rebel Captain's Royalist Bride — Anne Herries

MEDICAL

Her Hard to Resist Husband — Tina Beckett
The Rebel Doc Who Stole Her Heart — Susan Carlisle
From Duty to Daddy — Sue MacKay
Changed by His Son's Smile — Robin Gianna
Mr Right All Along — Jennifer Taylor
Her Miracle Twins — Margaret Barker

Discover more romance at

www.millsandboon.co.uk

- ❤ WIN great prizes in our exclusive competitions

- ❤ BUY new titles before they hit the shops

- ❤ BROWSE new books and REVIEW your favourites

- ❤ SAVE on new books with the Mills & Boon® Bookclub™

- ❤ DISCOVER new authors

PLUS, to chat about your favourite reads, get the latest news and find special offers:

- 📘 Find us on facebook.com/millsandboon
- 🐦 Follow us on twitter.com/millsandboonuk
- ❤ Sign up to our newsletter at millsandboon.co.uk